MIKE

BROTHERHOOD PROTECTORS WORLD

REGAN BLACK

Twisted Page Press LLC

BROTHERHOOD PROTECTORS

ORIGINAL SERIES BY ELLE JAMES

With special thanks to Elle James for inviting me into her world of Brotherhood Protectors

ABOUT GUARDIAN AGENCY: MIKE

When hope is lost, truth is blurred, and your life is on the line, it's time to call in the Guardian Agency...

Actress Lauren Marie Woods just witnessed her agent's murder. Now his killer is after her and the police are sure she pulled the trigger. More alone than ever in Hollywood, Lauren needs the kind of help only the elite Guardian Agency can provide.

Mike Stone is beyond jaded when it comes to actresses and Hollywood. But one thing is immediately clear: rising star Lauren Marie Woods will end up dead without his help. The real question is whether or not the former Navy SEAL can guard his heart from the beautiful actress.

Lauren must give the performance of her life to survive and help Mike catch the killer. But what will it take to crack the tough shell of the man who makes her want far more than his protection?

Author note: Previously published as *Too Far Gone*, this novel has been updated and revised for your enjoyment.

Visit ReganBlack.com for a full list of titles, excerpts and upcoming release dates. For early access to new releases, exclusive prizes, and much more, subscribe to Regan's monthly newsletter.

PROLOGUE

Relaxing on his surfboard, Mike Stone floated out in the Pacific Ocean, watching the water for one last good wave to ride into shore. He started most days out here, breathing the salt-tinged air and feeling the ocean move him. The habit kept his mind level, his body fit and ready.

He felt the wave he wanted driving closer and popped up on his board, riding the powerful curl until it spit him out near the shore. Wading in, he shook out his hair and let the wind dry him off as he walked to the battered Jeep he kept running just for surfing.

Securing his board, he climbed into the driver's seat and immediately reached into the lock box for his cell phone. He cringed at the flashing light of a waiting message. As a Guardian Agent bodyguard, he was expected to be accessible and ready to answer at all times.

The hour he allowed for surfing was the only time he was away from his phone. He checked the text message and relaxed. Instead of the single-word command of 'protect' that indicated a new assignment, this message was from Hank Patterson, a friend and fellow Navy SEAL, retired.

Seemed Hank was going to be in town for a few days while his wife Sadie, an A-list actress, dealt with some business. Mike replied immediately with a couple of times and suggestions for places they could relax.

It would be great catching up with one of the few who understood life after the adrenaline-rush of SEAL teams.

CHAPTER 1

West Hollywood, California
Tuesday, December 9, 5:45 p.m.

Lauren Marie Woods finished reading the script and turned it upside down on the small table as if hiding the title page would somehow make the entire mess go away. She'd chosen to read through the project alone and in public at a popular diner. It was the most effective way to keep her reactions—good or bad—in check. In Hollywood someone was always watching, eager to take an embarrassing photo or to start rumors that stirred up trouble.

Everyone interested in success played the game, but she preferred to go about it more quietly than most. Lauren saved the drama for the set instead of allowing it to seep into every nook and cranny of her personal life. According to her agent, Desmond Trinity, that was part of the problem. Desmond insisted her need for privacy was the reason her career wasn't punching the right high points. If only she'd cut loose occasionally, seek out some bad-girl publicity, and develop her inner diva, she would be in demand.

On that, they disagreed. Lauren believed there were better ways to stand out than a creating a trumped up drug charge at Hollywood's hotspot of the week or throwing a bogus tantrum on Rodeo Drive. Lauren wanted to be known as the impeccable professional among her peers. She cultivated a reputation as a dedicated and competent actress that directors and producers could count on. Everyone in town knew she showed up on day one and gave her best effort until the project wrapped. Still, she consistently got offers from directors who wanted nothing more than her generous curves on screen or her ability to scream on cue in low-budget horror films.

In time, Lauren had pinned down the real problem: Desmond. Her agent, and on-again-off-again boyfriend, never suggested her for more substantive projects. Sure, she held the choice role as fan-favorite Dr. Loveless on the Harper Cove daytime drama. She and Desmond agreed one hundred percent on the benefit of steady work. For her, it was the security of the paycheck padding her bank account and for Desmond, her success on the show boosted his talent agency's reputation.

Trinity Talent represented some of the top television and film stars. She'd been luckier than most new faces in Hollywood when she'd shown up ten years ago at the tender age of eighteen and landed his representation. He'd arranged her first auditions and she'd been working regularly almost from day one. Truly a stellar success story for a girl from small-town Kansas.

She glared at the offensive waste of paper on the table. With this script, far from stellar, Desmond had done it again, damn him. He'd told her this could be her breakout role, but obviously he'd been referring to her ability to break out of a demon's lair wearing only skimpy underwear. Why couldn't he—just once—support *her* vision for her career?

She gazed through the diner window at the glittering city lights along Sunset Strip until the surge of anger eased. Her arrival in Los Angeles had been like all those lights: bright and exciting, full of hope and dreams. If she wanted to push her career to the next level it was clearly time to sever her contract with Trinity Talent. The task would have been far simpler if she hadn't allowed their relationship to become personal along the way.

Not for the first time, she regretted giving in to his romantic overtures all those years ago. He'd been charming and smooth, and she'd been young and naïve. Lust and a grudging mutual respect weren't a solid foundation for love and weren't nearly enough to change Desmond. Without her role as Dr. Loveless and the self-imposed psychology research that went along with it, they wouldn't have lasted six months under the same roof. The research allowed her to deal with the highs and lows without losing her mind. Too bad her long-running performance as the 'adoring girlfriend of Desmond Trinity' would never be recognized with an Emmy or Oscar award.

Angry again—with both of them—it seemed her inner diva was suddenly willing to burst into the limelight with a world-class fit. What a scene it would be if she indulged the urge. For a moment, she imagined it. She could call him to meet her here, pour coffee over the useless script and toss it in his face. She had worked too hard, invested too much in her career to keep playing the bombshell screamer or ditzy girl-next-door. She wanted *real* roles. She wanted to dig into substantial parts that her fans would embrace.

Desmond was at the top of the echelon in Hollywood, and he consistently found those roles for other clients. For reasons he refused to explain, he'd never sent her to an audition for a part that had the potential to lift her out of the current rut and onto the A-list. He had several big-name clients and she understood she wasn't right for every script that crossed his desk. Still, as the longstanding man in her life, she'd expected a certain level of emotional commitment and professional support.

After all this time he had to know it wasn't about fame or being more popular than other actresses, not for her anyway. The more meaningful roles would allow her to grow creatively and provide the challenge she craved. She tapped her French manicured nails on the script. Obviously, he had no intention of opening his eyes as either her agent or her boyfriend. Or maybe he was afraid she'd outgrow him and move on. Either way, he was cheating her. And cheating on her. Again.

The headache was familiar. The dull ache somewhere in the vicinity of her heart surprised her. It wasn't heartache as much as a tangled glob of regret. No matter, she would need to tread carefully through the inevitable confrontation. Their personal relationship, like their business contract, served a purpose. She'd known for years they weren't living a love for the ages. Their time together would hardly meet the definition of mutual adoration, even in Hollywood. On some level, she'd stayed with Desmond for the visibility. His inability to stay faithful had killed her feelings for him long ago.

She'd been smart to handle this read-through of the script alone. If she'd agreed to his request to read it with him in the office tonight over dinner, she would've flung the script at him in a fit of temper, and then gone straight home to pack up and leave him. A stunt like that would've hit the tabloids within hours—he would've seen to that—pushing her further from her goals. Maybe that's what he wanted pushing this script on her. Everyone, even Desmond, had a tendency to assume her famous scream, glorious blond hair, and naturally large breasts negated her critical thinking skills.

Let them underestimate her. She was a good actress who could be great. Desmond knew it. Tonight, she'd seize the reins and take her career in the right direction. She'd dallied too long as it was. The security of his representation and a highly sought after home address no longer felt like the priority it once had.

Lauren paid her bill, leaving a generous tip for the waitress. She'd been there once, working every possible shift between casting calls until Desmond had found her and signed her.

She sighed. It was frustrating to feel so thankful to a man who'd let her down so often. But he'd given her a good start even if he refused to entertain her more serious plans for the future. For giving her that good start, she owed him a clean, civil break.

She rehearsed her speech aloud on the drive to his office on Wilshire Boulevard. He should be wrapping up his day by now. Desmond often filled his afternoons with interviewing—and screwing—the next generation of red-carpet wannabes. That was the primary reason their personal relationship had never made it to the next level. Lauren couldn't even remember the last time they'd shared a bed, much less made love. Deep down, she'd always considered Desmond more friend than boyfriend. Wouldn't he be shocked that his current girlfriend and client was done being a doormat?

On the street in front of the building, a glossy black car with dark windows took up both parking spaces assigned to Trinity Talent. Had Desmond planned to take her out to dinner? Maybe he, too, had realized a public place was best for this reading and the inevitable heated discussion. He had to know she wasn't going to be happy with the script. Then again, she was early. Maybe he had an appointment. If he was in there banging some new bimbo, she might just pitch one of those famous Hollywood fits after all.

Lauren found a parking spot just around the corner and turned off the engine. Flipping down the visor, she checked her make-up and freshened her lip gloss. He often said her mouth was one of his favorite features and she wanted him to have some regrets about treating her this way. If he was taking her to dinner, the casual floral skirt, snug sweater, and heels might not pack the right punch. For a moment she considered going by the house to change into a power suit like those worn by her Dr. Loveless character.

No. She'd put this off too long already. She needed to do this here and now, before she lost her nerve. Mentally reciting her speech one more time, a new way to play it popped into her mind. Silence might be golden. A note would drive home her point and, depending on who he might be entertaining, could prevent a rash of rumors.

With the script in her lap, she searched her car console, her purse, and then beneath the passenger seat until she found a working pen. She wrote only two words 'We're done' in the blank space under the title. Then she signed her name. Knowing Desmond, he'd auction her autograph on the web. Still, the note was better than opening the door for him to beg for one more chance.

Locking the car, she dropped her keys into her purse, and slung it over her shoulder before heading for the side door of the building. "Actors and actresses change agents all the time. No big deal." The news would make the usual rag papers and magazines, but eventually it would be replaced by some other actor's latest move or dilemma.

Head held high, she summoned the posture and poise of her Dr. Loveless character on her way to the lobby elevators. She poked the call button and took a long, deep breath. "Hand him the script and walk away," she reminded herself in a whisper. They could divvy up their classic movie collection later. Clean. Civil. A no-drama breakup. Just two people going their separate ways.

Rolling and unrolling the script in her hands, her impatience ratcheted up. She pushed the call button again but neither elevator seemed inclined to cooperate. She blew out a big breath. One way or another she was going to finish this tonight. She turned on her heel and headed for the stairs.

Desmond would protest and try sweet-talking her. He would promise and cajole, but deflecting all that would be the easy part. The challenge would be maintaining her composure in the face of his inevitable explosive lecture touting his expertise and long-range vision for her. She clutched the script in her fist, a tangible reminder of what was at stake.

"We're done," she whispered. Whatever it took, she would make him believe it. She would not tolerate any more of his bravado and bluster.

When she reached the fourth floor, she decided to use one last advantage and headed for the back entrance to the office suite. Desmond used this rear exit when he wanted to slip away unnoticed from a waiting client. As she passed the break room where Desmond's lovely assistant prepped perfect, calorie-controlled refreshments for his clients during regular business hours, she heard raised voices, though she couldn't make out the words. She eased closer. The door was open but she couldn't see inside. It sounded like everyone involved was male.

"Wait!" Desmond shouted, his voice tight with desperation.

"We are *done* waiting," the man replied in a flat

voice of indeterminate European origin. "You have failed to fulfill our requirements."

Desmond must be helping someone rehearse, Lauren decided. Wanting a better look, she tiptoed a little closer to the open door.

"Not a failure, gentlemen. A hiatus," Desmond's voice was smoother, though still laced with tension. "A short pause, that's all. The feds have been sniffing around. Believe me, I'm protecting everyone's interests."

"You offer me excuses? You are weak. Useless!"

Lauren was near enough now to see two men in dark suits facing off with Desmond. The shorter one doing all the talking seemed to be in charge. From this angle it was impossible to see more than a glimpse of their profiles. The man in charge nodded and the second man, this one a little younger and taller, stepped forward. If this was a rehearsal, where were the scripts?

"Let's all take a big breath and relax," Desmond implored taking a step back. His tie was loose and his suit jacket was askew on his shoulders. "You know I always come through."

Definitely not a rehearsal. She'd never seen him so disheveled in a client meeting.

"If I give you time, when will we have the product you promised?" the shorter man demanded.

"Patience is a virtue," Desmond replied, visibly regaining his composure. "As soon as the feds get distracted, I'll have the cream of the crop delivered. Andreas knows I'm good for it."

"If Mr. Polzin had any confidence in you, *I* would not be here." The shorter man spat on the floor, and then gave another nod. The taller man drove a fist into Desmond's stomach. He doubled over only to take a hard elbow to the kidneys.

Lauren jumped. Her heart stumbled. What was going on here?

"I give you my word," Desmond sputtered between gasps for breath.

"That is not good enough, Mr. Trinity."

A kick to his midsection had Desmond collapsing at the boss's feet. A muffled scream jerked Lauren's attention beyond the men to the couch on far side of the office. A beautiful woman only half dressed cowered there. Her eyes were wide, her thick mane of dark hair tousled. Anger momentarily burned through the Lauren's fear. So Desmond had been here with a fledgling actress. The woman looked older than the typical wannabe and vaguely familiar, but—

"Our patience has run out," the boss was saying. "We require the best product on schedule to maintain our reputation and to keep the money flowing. Money you like to spend, no?"

Desmond peered up at the man. "Yes. Yes. I understand. I'll make it happen. Just give me a chance."

Lauren had to do something. She reached into her purse, searched for her phone. Not there. Her pocket! She'd put it in her pocket at the diner. She dug into her pocket. Empty. Damn it! She must've dropped it in the car. She glanced back down the corridor. There wasn't a phone in the break room. What could she do? Maybe if she interrupted the meeting she could cool things down.

The boss was speaking again. "Mr. Trinity, Mr. Polzin would like me to inform you that your services are no longer required." He brushed one palm against the other. "You are finished."

Lauren took a breath and prepared to announce herself. When she opened her mouth to speak she saw the gun. Her mouth snapped shut on a scream as her heart launched into her throat. The taller man bent down and pressed the menacing barrel of a hand gun to the back of Desmond's head. Before she could blink, he'd fired. Twice. The quick pops hissed in the eerie silence. Desmond's body jerked once and then slumped lifeless to the floor.

A low, keening wail filled the office as the woman on the couch lost it.

The boss shook his head. "Shut her up."

The script fell from Lauren's hands. At the sound, the boss swiveled around. For what felt like an eternity, they stared at each other. Dark hair slicked back from his high forehead, heavy eyebrows over hollow, dark eyes, hooked nose, and thin mouth. The image was seared into her memory.

"Well, well," the boss said, "who do we have here?"

Lauren bolted.

She heard him snap out orders in a foreign language. His calm terrified her even more. She made it to the stairwell, her heels clattering on the treads. Stumbling at the third floor landing, she heard heavy footsteps on the stairs above. Every nerve in her body quaked and her hands slipped on the door handle as she rushed out of the stairwell and into a maze of shorter corridors.

She'd call 911 from one of the offices and hide until help arrived. She tested one door after another, all of them locked. She refused to go out like this.

"Stop running and I will be easy on you." The words echoed through the darkness.

As if she would believe something so absurd. They'd killed Desmond and the woman, too, probably. Why would they keep her alive? Trembling, she tore off her shoes and moved faster. One of these doors had to be open.

"You are a beautiful woman, Lauren Marie."

When the boss spoke, his voice seemed to float all around her, a menacing cloud. Of course he knew her name. He knew Desmond. Most likely, he knew where they lived. She had to get down to the lobby—

"I know how to care for beautiful women. Come

to me, and I will put the world at your feet. I am far more powerful than your dead lover."

She struggled to think beyond the smothering panic. She had to *do* something.

"Nikoli?" the man called out, his persistent footfalls echoing softly on the hard floors. Coming closer.

"Here."

Dear, God! They had spread out. With all the offices locked, the two of them would have her cornered soon. There had to be an option, a choice that didn't end with her dead.

She looked around for anything she could use as a weapon. Spotting the fire alarm on the wall, she made her way there and pulled it. The alarm clanged and emergency lights flashed up and down the hallways. Water from the sprinklers in the ceiling drenched the hallway. Taking the fire extinguisher, she hid behind the nearby water cooler.

Somewhere down the corridor the men were swearing, the words a cruel accompaniment to the jarring flashes of the strobing lights. "Wrong choice, Lauren Marie!" the boss shouted. "You are a dead woman!"

She gripped the fire extinguisher, her body shaking. Suddenly she heard sirens wailing outside. Hope swelled in her chest, but the silence in the corridor had her pulse galloping even harder. Where were the killers? Had they decided she wasn't worth the risk of getting caught? Did she dare hope they cut their losses and run?

Every second of the next two or three minutes pounded like a hammer, each one etched in her mind. Thudding boots and new voices gave her the courage to peek past the water cooler. Firefighters hustled along the corridor.

Trembling so hard she dropped the fire extinguisher, Lauren moved away from her hiding place. At the noise, the firefighter closest to her stopped short, the beam of his flashlight blinding her.

"Please." She held up her hands. "Please, help me."

WILSHIRE BOULEVARD POLICE PRECINCT, 11:38 p.m.

"That's it?" As exhausted and emotionally weary as Lauren was, she felt stunned at the detective's indifference. They were sending her home without any assurances or protection.

"These things take time," the detective said.

Time? "I've spent the last three hours explaining how Desmond was murdered by those men in his office. I can't believe they let the woman live. I've given descriptions to your sketch artist. I've cooperated with your every request, including having *my* hands checked for gunpowder residue. Now you expect me to just walk out of here as if two killers aren't looking for me?"

This was insane!

Detective Randolph Treadwell shrugged. "If anyone gives you any trouble—" he nodded toward the business card she held "—give me a call."

"The killers saw me. They *chased* me." Anger and fear churned wildly deep inside her belly. "They know my name. What I saw. How long do you think it will take them to find me?"

Treadwell leaned back from the interview table. He'd loosened his tie and lost the suit coat hours ago. Everything about the middle-aged man screamed impatience. He was ready to go home and Lauren was the last hurdle standing in his way.

"Look, Miss Woods, you have my word we're doing all we can to find your boyfriend's killer. But the fact of the matter is, unlike TV cops, our resources are limited. If you need us, call. That's the best I can do."

Lauren stood. "Fine."

Treadwell pushed back his chair and stood as well. "If you think of anything else, be sure to let me know. And don't leave town. We may have follow-up questions."

Because staying in town was smart when a killer knew your name and address, and possibly everything else. That urge to throw a fit was rising again. "What about the woman in the office with Desmond? Who was she?"

He scratched his forehead. "Guess I forgot to

mention the only body we found was your boyfriend's."

"That's impossible. The man who ordered Desmond's murder told the second man to shut her up." Had there been a third gunshot? She closed her eyes and instantly regretted it as the memory of Desmond's body and the killer's face popped into her mind. Was it possible they hadn't killed her? Lauren wrapped her arms around her stomach. Had she left that woman to fend for herself?

Treadwell shrugged. "We found no visible indication anyone else was in the office. Fact is, we'll be analyzing evidence and going through finger print databases for days, but right now it's just your story and a dead body."

She got the distinct impression he'd saved this bombshell just to gauge her reaction. The rant was building in her throat. She was a witness to *murder*. He'd reduced her relationship with Desmond to something sleazy and now he practically accused her of lying. "Are we done here?" she asked through gritted teeth.

"For now," Treadwell said. "Officer Cooper will see you to your car."

Lauren couldn't get out of the room fast enough. She was grateful it was Cooper, the first officer on the scene, walking her out. He was the only cop she'd encountered tonight who'd been nice to her.

Following Cooper toward the precinct entrance,

she tried again to pin down where she'd seen the woman in Desmond's office. She knew that face. Whatever it was, it niggled at the back of her mind. Then again, she crossed paths with dozens of other actresses every week. Maybe it would come to her. Lauren prayed the woman wasn't dead or being held hostage. How could she have just left her there?

Replaying it over and over, Lauren knew any other choice would have gotten her killed.

"Treadwell can be a jerk, but he knows his stuff," Cooper said as they walked to her car. "He closes cases."

"I'm glad it's only his people skills that are lacking." Whatever business Desmond had been conducting, he deserved justice. So did the woman who was likely guilty of nothing more than being in the wrong place at the wrong time.

Cooper hesitated at the driver's side door of her car. "Do you have a private security team or a bodyguard, Miss Woods?"

She sighed. She was so damned tired. "Desmond…" Her voice cracked on his name. "He suggested it a few times, but I never followed through." A lack of follow through summed up their entire relationship. "It's never been an issue." Until now.

"Maybe this will help." Cooper handed her a business card.

"The Guardian Agency?" She studied the gold

shield logo centered over a website address and toll free phone number.

"It's a private group. The best. They might be more help than the department right now. They helped a good friend of mine."

"Thank you, Officer Cooper." Finding her keys, she hit the unlock button on the fob.

Cooper opened her door. "You take care now." When she'd settled behind the steering wheel, he closed the door and gave a wave before walking away.

Lauren slowly buckled her seat belt, wondering what to do and where to go next. She couldn't bear the idea of hiding with a friend and putting that person in jeopardy. She stared at the business card.

What did she have to lose?

CHAPTER 2

VENICE BEACH, California
   Wednesday, December 10, 5:30 a.m.

MIKE STONE JERKED awake and struggled to draw air into his lungs. He closed his eyes as the sound of children screaming echoed over and over before fading with the images that still haunted him. "Just a nightmare," he muttered. He was in California, not Mumbai.

Damn. Would *nothing* work? He'd hoped the time spent jawing with Hank last night would dull the bite of those memories.

His cell phone, set to vibrate, rattled against his nightstand and he dragged his thoughts back to the present. Rubbing the sleep from his eyes, he picked it up and read the single word on the display: Protect.

He adjusted the pillow under his head and waited for the rest of the assignment. In the pre-dawn darkness outside his window the Pacific Ocean crashed into the sand. There went his plans for a long run on the beach followed by his standing morning date with the waves. Well, hell. He sat up and rolled his shoulders, cracked his neck. A shower and a bottle of cola would have to suffice today. Moments later the picture came through along with the primary background on the new client.

Well, hello, beautiful. The client was gorgeous, one serious perk of working this part of the country. He skimmed through her file, not at all surprised that face had landed steady work on a daytime soap in addition to several commercials and small-movie roles.

Mike's curiosity spiked as he read the first notes. She'd witnessed her talent agent's murder. The killer had seen her and given chase, but she'd managed to escape. The police, in all their wisdom, had taken her statement, sat her down with a sketch artist, and sent her on her way.

If the hit was professional, why was she still alive? Mike supposed miracles happened, though he'd never seen one personally. How she survived wasn't the issue. She'd asked the Guardian Agency for protection and he would deliver.

Another text came through: Urgent!

"Aren't they all?" Mike muttered at the phone as

he entered the contact number provided for the client.

It rang twice before the woman answered with a wary hello.

"Mike Stone, Guardian Agency," he said. "Is this Lauren Marie Woods?"

"Oh, thank God," she said in a breathless rush. "Yes, this is Lauren and I'm in big trouble."

Got that loud and clear. "Are you in a safe location?"

"Yes. I-I think so. I'm in a motel near LAX." She gave him the name and address.

"Stay there until I arrive."

"H-how far away ar-are you?" The stutter in her voice revealed just how scared she was. Then again, she was an actress by trade.

Mike checked his watch, thought about routes and the light traffic at this hour. "Give me forty-five minutes."

"Okay. How will I know it's you?"

Fair question. "I'll send you a head shot. See you soon." He ended the call and took a selfie. It wouldn't win artistic awards for subject or composition, but it would serve as identification.

Mike dressed quickly, grabbed his go-bag, and headed for the car he used for cases. Once he was settled behind the wheel, the deep rumble of the Camaro's engine gave him almost as much pleasure as surfing and smoothed out the rough edges of another restless night. One day he'd find a way to purge these damned nightmares for good.

The streets were mostly clear and the sun no more than a whisper of light at the horizon, giving him time to think. A dangerous pastime when a guy couldn't get his mind off what he couldn't change. "What's done is done," he muttered. He was here now. His career as a Navy SEAL was over. No going back.

Without the steady work as a Guardian Agency protector, Mike would still be banging through odd jobs and squeaking by as a bounty hunter. His gaze drifted west toward the ocean as he headed inland. Only two things pulled him out of a crappy mood these days. Surfing or a case. Surfing kept his mind and body sharp. Being a protector bolstered his self-respect, gave him a purpose. Not a bad recipe for success for a washed out, retired SEAL.

Checking the time on the dash, he used the buttons on the steering wheel to cue the voice commands so the new client's file would be read aloud. He smiled as the automated voice based on Claudia, his Guardian Agency technical assistant, filled the car. The expression faded as he concentrated on the background. Woods was a college dropout from Kansas. She'd been in Hollywood for a decade, working consistently. Impressive. Her primary personal ties included associates from her daytime soap and a long-term relationship with her agent—also known as the victim.

Mike thought of her desperate, pleading voice. The past few hours must've been harrowing, yet she was still alive. Takes smarts and creativity to stay a step ahead of a serious death threat. And from what Claudia provided, the hit Woods' had witnessed had been professional. He played and replayed the transcript of her request for Guardian Agency assistance, piecing the scene together in his mind.

A few minutes early for the meet at her motel, he searched the immediate area carefully. He found her car parked close to the side entrance, but didn't see anyone who might be keeping an eye on it. He wasn't quite ready to call that a good omen. Scared enough to stay away from home, he wondered if Miss Woods had been smart enough to pay cash or offer a false ID when she checked in. By the look of it, he wasn't sure this particular motel took anything but cash.

Parking as close to the front door as possible, he weighed his options for the initial meeting. He reached over and pulled a snub-nosed revolver out of the glove box. Sliding the gun into his shoulder holster, he left the car and headed inside, striding past the front desk without being noticed. Not good. He took the stairs to the third floor. According to his watch, he was six minutes ahead of schedule. Before he could knock the door opened.

At first glance, the brunette staring at him looked

nothing like the knockout blond in the case file. In jeans, a snug sweater, and with feet bare, she was shorter than he'd expected, but he recognized the striking, silver-blue eyes. She examined his face, then her gaze skimmed down to his shoes and back up again.

"You're early, Mr. Stone."

"A little." He kept his hands visible. "Can I come in?"

"ID?" she asked, showing no signs of the distress he'd heard over the phone.

He slowly reached for his wallet and flipped it open for her inspection.

She gave it a study and, with a nod, stepped back from the door allowing him to enter the room.

"Thank you." He turned, flipping the u-lock and deadbolt into place. He looked around the room, assessing the closed curtains, the television tuned to a local station, an overnight bag, and her purse. "Can you walk me through your situation? I've read your file, but it's always good to hear the details firsthand."

"Okay." Her pink-tipped toes curled into the carpet. "Is it typical for bounty hunters to moonlight in personal security?"

How did she know about that? "I'm not sure what you mean."

"I'm sorry." She twisted her hands together. "Let me explain. I have an excellent memory for faces. As soon as I received your selfie I knew I'd seen you before. You stood in the background during the press conferences when the Angeles Forest killer was found and brought back for trial."

How the hell did she remember that? The case had played out two years ago? "The county sheriff did excellent work on that one." He couldn't think about that capture or he'd give her an earful that would violate the gag order on the case.

"With your help, right?"

He braced his hands on his hips. "Are you interviewing me?" That wasn't how things worked. Another upside of working for the Guardian Agency was the knowledge that he was employed by the best in the business. "If so, you should be aware I don't do the sharing thing. If you want to know how good I am, check the Guardian Agency's reputation. If that doesn't satisfy you, I suggest you rethink your strategy."

"Sore spot," she said. "No problem, I'll leave it alone. You're better looking in person, by the way."

Mike shook his head. He had a feeling all this rambling was a sign of just how nervous the lady was. "And you weren't a brunette in the file photo," he countered. Had she cut and dyed her hair or was the original picture the façade? In Hollywood it could go either way.

"Do you prefer blondes?" Her full mouth tilted at one corner as she reached up and tugged off the brunette wig, allowing a tumble of long blond hair to fall loose. "I can do that. Well, it seems." A hint of sadness weighted her last statement.

All that lush hair falling around her shoulders would've been an enticing distraction under different circumstances. He typically got a read on his clients immediately, but her tone and body language were all over the place. Maybe it went with the territory in the acting business. At any rate, it posed a new set of variables and potential problems. He put another mental checkmark in the 'not good' column.

"Your personal vehicle is parked outside," he began, determined to stay focused. "Did you check in here under your real name?"

"Yes and no."

"Miss Woods, I don't tolerate games. I prefer straight answers."

"It's not a game." She pushed her hands through her hair, smoothing it back from her face. "I saw two men murder Desmond Trinity last night. They know I can identify them and the police don't seem to care." She inhaled a big breath. "Do you want coffee?" she asked, gesturing to the small personal coffee maker.

"No, thanks." She was definitely a ball of nerves. "Maybe we should sit down."

She shook her head. "I can't sit still right now."

"Fine." He took the desk chair, hoping the example would rub off on her. "How did you register for the room?"

"I have an agency credit card and ID as Marie

Woodson on Desmond's corporate account. Sometimes it's nice when no one knows who you are."

"I see." He hitched a thumb toward the discarded wig. "And you carry disguises with you regularly?"

Her frown turned to a scowl. "I needed a disguise so I stopped by the studio and grabbed a few things. The night watchman was happy to let me in. It was the best I could do on short notice."

He had to hand it to the lady, for someone who'd witnessed a murder and barely escaped the same fate, she'd pulled it together admirably.

She passed her cell phone to him. "You can scroll through those," she suggested. "I took pictures of the sketches the artist drew. Those two men were arguing with Desmond when I arrived—"

"Your boyfriend," he suggested. The file had said long-term personal relationship.

She winced. "Sort of. He's—he *was*—my agent. I'd gone to the office to tell him I was done with him personally and professionally, but those men were there. I witnessed everything from just outside his office door."

Mike studied the faces of the two men, both in dark suits. She'd had the bulkier man drawn without a tie. Looked like a boss and his muscle. The third sketch was a woman. She was slim and exotic with lots of hair, maybe a couple of years older than his new client. "How is she involved?" Mike asked, turning the phone toward Lauren.

"I have no idea. She was in the office. I assume she's Desmond's latest acquisition. Or fling. Or she was going to be one or both. I've seen her somewhere, but I can't put my finger on it."

"All right." Deciding they were safe enough for the moment, he returned her phone. "Sit down and walk me through what happened."

She dropped onto the edge of the mattress and slowly related the events. He was impressed when she delivered the story in a steady voice. "You have no idea what product they were talking about?"

She shook her head.

"Hold on." He reached for the television remote. Breaking news about the case filled the screen behind her.

LAUREN STARED at the television as the reporter's voice filled the room.

"LAPD officials announced an eye-witness came forward early this morning," the reporter said. "The witness has provided a full account of Desmond Trinity's murder. Combined with evidence gathered at the scene, the police have named Lauren Marie Woods a person of interest and will be questioning her later today."

"That's... impossible." Lauren shook her head. "No one else was there."

Desmond's floor as well as the one below it had been empty. The memory of rushing from one locked door to the next flashed through her mind. She'd been reliving it all night. The image on the screen changed to a helicopter view and her stomach dropped. Police cars had converged in front of Desmond's house and two men in suits, flanked by two uniformed officers, were striding up the walk. News crews and anyone with a camera seemed to be crowding the front lawn.

"You must have expected reporters and paparazzi," Stone said. "Aren't they always following you around?"

"Not as much as you'd think." She could hardly hear her voice over the buzzing in her ears. "I'm not on top of the A-list like Desmond." She shook her head. "I don't understand this." She stared at Stone. "Who could have come forward?"

"Let's talk about the woman you saw last night," he offered. "Is it possible she's the new witness? Maybe she hid while the bad guys were chasing you."

"Maybe?" She rubbed at her aching temples. "I *will* remember her. I always do. It's like when you hear a snippet of a song and you just can't remember the title or artist, but then it suddenly comes to you in a satisfying flash."

Like the selfie he'd sent this morning had given her a surprise rush of anticipation, beyond knowing help was imminent. His eyes, that dark, mesmerizing blue, had lit a spark of interest deep inside her. His strong jaw shadowed with a day's beard growth stirred up something she didn't know she'd been missing. That he was tall and built like an Olympic swimmer was icing on the cake. She gave herself a mental kick and pushed aside that last part. Apparently her mind was seeking any possible relief from the tension. According to her psychology research that was what people did in desperate situations.

She could see he didn't have much confidence in her claim. "At the press conference you hadn't shaved for at least two days," she told him. "You had mud on your jeans and your field jacket was dusty. Your hands were scraped up. Odds are low that happened in the sheriff's station."

"You might be surprised," he argued, but she didn't miss the glint of respect in his eyes.

She pressed her point. "The sheriff's uniform was pressed and clean as he soaked up the praise and hogged the spotlight, taking credit for a capture you obviously handled. They barely mentioned your service as a Navy SEAL. Pretty obvious to me, you made the rescue."

He shrugged. "That wasn't a one-man job," he said. "And the Navy would prefer it if no one mentioned my name and the SEAL teams in the same sentence."

She'd much rather talk about him, if only her situation hadn't just gone from bad to worse. She needed to focus. "The detective in charge of the case called my cell several times before he finally left a voicemail. He didn't mention a new witness. I was afraid to take a call from anyone until you arrived." Thank God she'd followed her intuition. Could the police really believe she was a person of interest? "Do you think the reporter is using my name for ratings?"

"We'll know the answer to that soon enough. If they're calling your cell and moving on your house, I'd rather talk more once we relocate somewhere safer."

"I can't go into hiding. We need to find her." Lauren's options had evaporated. If the woman was alive and the witness the police claimed, then she could confirm Lauren's story. If the witness was someone planted by the killer, the police were being manipulated and Lauren was in more trouble than before.

"My job is to protect you, Miss Woods." He relaxed in the chair, those striking midnight-blue eyes scrutinizing her with an intensity that defied his nonchalant posture. "Life isn't like the movies or a soap opera. You've managed to evade a killer for a few hours, but the police are now searching for you, too. Those thugs who shot your boyfriend—"

"Agent," she reminded him, irritated.

"Whatever," he dismissed the clarification. "The killer can sit back and let the police do the legwork. The bad guys can take you out once you're in custody. During a transfer or even when you're behind bars."

His warning sent a tremor skittering down her spine even as his arrogance rankled. She couldn't argue with the facts. Her mind raced, searching for a feasible alternative.

"The police will sift through everything in Trinity's office," he was saying. "When they find the records, your alternate ID becomes a neon sign. Unless you have cash tucked away somewhere or a friend with a private island, you won't last a week outside a safe house."

"I'll find a way." She couldn't go into hiding. However badly Desmond had treated her and ignored her career, he had helped her as well. She would not turn her back on him without at least trying to find his killer and clear her name. Lauren had some cash on her. "I'm not an idiot, Mr. Stone. I have resources and I'll come up with a plan, with or without your help."

"You have resources that won't turn on you?" He stood up and stepped toward her. "Resources that can circumvent the police from railroading you into a murder charge?" Another step closer, crowding her. "Resources willing to take an accessory rap if they're caught aiding your escape when your status goes from person of interest to suspect?"

She struggled to breathe around the hard lump in her throat. There were people in her life she trusted, but if any of them got hurt or jailed because of her…

"That's enough." She held up a hand. She *would* find a way.

He halted his advance but he was already in her personal space, his gaze unyielding. "You're willing to take the chance your resources could be killed for helping you?"

No. "Stop." She barely resisted the urge to cover her ears. She would never forgive herself if she involved a friend who got hurt because of her.

"The way I see it, you're well and truly caught between killers and cops. You can't afford to ignore my advice," Stone said.

He was right. The flare of worry in his eyes gave her a moment's pause. He was a stranger. Why would he care if she lived or died? The sterling reputation of his agency, of course. "I can't just hide," she said. "I have to find the woman. She's the one person who can back up my story and help me bring a killer to justice."

"Why?"

She glared at him. "Why what?"

"You just told me he wasn't your boyfriend." Stone folded his arms across his broad chest. "Why risk your life to bring his killer to justice?"

"You heard the reporter." She pointed at the television. "I'm a person of interest. I need proof of my story so the police can't railroad me or my career and possibly my life are over."

"The burden of proof is on them, Miss Woods. All you really need to do is stay alive until they figure out the truth. Making sure you stay safe is *my* job. Let's go."

"For how long? What if the police don't find the killers? What if they interpret everything through the lens that I'm guilty?" She'd never feel safe again until those two men were in jail.

Stone tilted his head toward the television. "Let's say the witness is the woman you saw last night, coerced by the bad guys who have decided to frame you."

"But it's a lie," she protested.

"Doesn't matter. They don't need her statement to hold up in court, they only need it to bring you into the open."

Staying alive was paramount, obviously. Her goals and dreams would hardly matter if she got killed for being stubborn. "You didn't answer my question. How long do I hide?"

He shrugged. "I don't have a crystal ball, Miss Woods. I'll help you keep your head down for as long as it takes."

Her knees gave out and she reached for the door to steady herself. Surviving this nightmare meant relying on the sexy, domineering man standing in front of her. She dried her clammy palms on her jeans.

"Okay." She surrendered to fate. For now. "Tell me what to do?"

"You're absolutely certain you didn't see anyone else at the scene?"

"No one else," she said.

"All right. Once you're safe, we can see about getting a look at the evidence and hopefully get a name of this supposed eye-witness."

"Any photos released will be on the gossip show circuits by tonight."

"Don't get your hopes up that they'll release the witness's name or photo. Time is our enemy. We need to get ahead of this before it spirals any further out of control." He pulled out his phone and sent an email or text message.

"What if I cooperate?" Lauren chewed her bottom lip as she considered the idea. "Surely I can talk to Detective Treadwell without being taken into custody."

"You don't need to talk to anyone but me right now. The people who took out your... agent may be part of an organized crime syndicate. Based on your descriptions, the accents, and names you heard, my money's on organized crime. Probably Russian. They don't leave loose ends. Particularly if they have reason to believe you know something."

He stared at her with an expectant expression, as if she should volunteer some new, enlightening detail. "I've told you. Last night was the first I'd seen either of those men. I have no idea why they wanted to kill Desmond or what the product is."

"You lived with Trinity, worked with him. There must've been some indication he was associated with something illegal."

Lauren knew that tone. It was the tone powerful men took all too often with her, assuming the pretty little lady had rocks in her head. Desmond had used it too many times, with her and others. She closed her eyes and thought of the ocean, of digging her toes into the sand as the tide kissed her feet. Some people said they felt small when staring out at the vastness of the ocean. Not her. She'd felt bigger and stronger from the first moment the Pacific Ocean had washed over her skin. The new awareness had been a monumental discovery when she'd arrived in California. On the beach, staring out over the endless stretch of water, she felt connected and infused with energy as if the ocean fueled her. Pulling deep from that well of calm strength, she opened her eyes once more.

"When I arrived in Hollywood, I worked my ass off. Desmond signed me for my looks and my work ethic. No casting couch. Our relationship was strictly professional at the start. He was a player and I knew it, but he was also one hell of an agent. Rumors aside, it took him *years* to convince me to take our relationship to a personal level, and a few more of blissful ignorance before I caught him cheating on me."

Stone cocked that handsome yet arrogant head of his. "Is there some point you're getting to?"

She refused to be goaded by his impatience. "This industry is ruthless, no matter how beautiful the people in front of the camera are. Reputation is everything and infidelity happens every day. If I'd thrown a tantrum about him sleeping with someone else it would've started a media feeding frenzy. I would've been out of the agency in a heartbeat, my career damaged—perhaps beyond repair."

She held up a finger when he started to interrupt her again. "Being faithful to Desmond has been my most challenging role, but I played it to perfection. Don't assume that means I knew every facet of his businesses. The opposite is true." The distance she had kept between them gave him plenty of room to do whatever or whomever he pleased. She could just imagine what Mr. Stone thought of her choices. Bodyguard or not, she owed him no explanations. "Whatever he was doing for or with those men, he didn't deserve to be murdered."

A muscle twitched in Stone's jaw. "All right. You have my word. I will do all I can to find the truth while protecting you. Put the wig back on. Grab the rest of your things and let's move."

Lauren nodded, uncertain whether she should be grateful or terrified. She gathered her few belongings and pulled out her car keys as they left the room.

"Give me your phone and your car key," he said as they reached the stairwell.

"Why?" She didn't appreciate the way he fired orders at her.

"They can use either or both to find you," he explained.

Reluctantly she handed over the items, telling herself it was temporary. They moved down the stairs quickly and then took the motel's side exit to avoid the lobby.

"To the right," he said. The lights on a Camaro flashed.

The sleek muscle car suited the man perfectly, she thought as he loaded her bag into the back seat. "I'd like to get my phone charger from my car. I might not need it now, but there's always later."

He heaved a patient sigh. "You get in, I'll grab your charger for later—much later."

"Fine." She climbed into the passenger seat, annoyed that he couldn't be bothered with a simple please. She felt like a boot camp trainee every time he barked at her. "Sit down. Get in. Give me your phone," she grumbled, mimicking his deep voice.

As he walked toward her car, he raised her key fob and clicked to unlock the doors. The lights flashed once and the entire car was engulfed in fire, the explosion deafening.

Lauren's heart slammed against her ribs. The concussive wave of the blast shoved at the Camaro and the shock that seized her was nearly as violent as the explosion. She curled in on herself as panic reigned.

The driver's side door of the Camaro opened and Mr. Stone dropped into the seat. "Buckle up. We're out of here."

She wanted to ask questions, but she couldn't speak through the fear. Instead, she watched the dark smoke from what had been her car rise into the morning sky. Her hands shook as she buckled her seatbelt. Her gaze settled on the man behind the wheel.

She might be dead right now if she hadn't listened to him.

CHAPTER 3

MIKE'S BRAIN kept replaying the fireball consuming her car. Whoever had killed Trinity was serious about tying up loose ends. It didn't matter that he and Lauren made a clean escape and were now pulling into the driveway of a Guardian Agency safe house. He couldn't erase the image from his mind. As a SEAL, he'd seen plenty of bombs, before and after detonation, in training and in the field. He'd used explosives and understood the process as well as the irrevocable damage inflicted on property and personnel.

He reviewed the whole scenario again from his arrival at the motel to their departure, and he couldn't pinpoint a surveillance detail. Whoever had planted the device had been long gone when he arrived. The obvious conclusion was someone had followed her to the motel last night. It was the only way they could have planted the bomb so quickly. It would have been the perfect cleanup strike. Tie up the loose end without getting too close.

"Where are we?" she asked. "Do you live here?"

"This is an agency safe house," he replied. "It's fully furnished and completely untraceable. You'll be safe here."

She peered through the windshield at the house. "Are you sure I shouldn't call Detective Treadwell?" She heaved a heavy breath. "Forget I asked. On some level I suspected he'd try and pin this on me."

What would it take to convince her that hiding was her best option? "You can make that call when we're ready to handle the fallout. I'm considering a couple of angles." That should buy him some thinking time and give him space to check in with Claudia. He should've updated her on the drive over, but making certain they weren't followed from the motel had required his full focus.

As if he'd telegraphed the thought, Mike's phone rang while he maneuvered the Camaro into the garage and cut the engine.

"Is your client secure?" Claudia asked.

"She is. Good morning to you, too," he teased.

Claudia grunted. "Chatter has increased across all news outlets."

"No kidding. You're on speaker by the way," he added. "The latest report we saw mentioned an eyewitness. The police want to bring my client in as a person of interest. I need to know what changed and who this witness is before I make any decisions."

"Anything else?"

In his mind, she was arching an eyebrow over tiny glasses and glaring at him like a perturbed librarian. "Not right now." In the background, he heard her chair creaking.

"Text me with your grocery list and I'll arrange delivery," she offered, ever one step ahead of him.

Though he'd never had a face to face with Claudia, Mike could imagine her workspace based on his military experience with technical personnel and communications experts. An array of monitors probably fanned out across a wide desk in a dim room. Like him, she was always available. He often wondered if she assisted any other protectors with the Agency.

"Who is that?" Lauren asked in a whisper.

"I'm Claudia, technical assistant for the Guardian Agency, Miss Woods. You'll have to excuse Mike, he has no manners."

Lauren gave him a look that suggested she agreed with Claudia.

"You have an ETA on that info?" he asked, eager to put a little distance between him and the lady—client—who kept his senses standing at attention. Despite being exhausted and scared, she refused to simply cave in to circumstances or direction. He respected that, even when it annoyed him. Add in her commitment to justice and he might be smitten if she wasn't a case.

"This is going to take some time," Claudia said. "I can get into the reporter's email service no problem, but dipping into the police server is a different matter. Keep your head down until I call you back."

She ended the call.

"So we lay low," Mike said, pushing open his door. "Don't worry, she's quick."

"There's nothing else we can do?" She grabbed her purse and climbed out.

He glanced at her across the roof of the car before reaching into the back seat for their bags. "We wait, yes. The house isn't a hardship, trust me."

"But..."

She looked lost. And all wrong as a brunette. He shook off the random thought. "You still have questions about how I'm doing the job you hired me to do?"

She shrugged. "I don't know, Mr. Stone."

He understood. She was overwhelmed and she needed to believe that good would prevail over evil. Lauren Marie Woods might not realize it but Hollywood veteran or not, she was still naïve about the way the world worked. "How about you call me Mike. Mr. Stone is my old man."

She nodded. "All right. Mike. So, what now?"

"Let's get settled and then we'll talk."

She released a big breath. "You're the boss."

A factor she was obviously less than pleased about. She was stressed out—with good reason. In her shoes he'd resist standing down too. "I'm here to keep you out of harm's way, Miss Woods," he reminded her. "You might not like my methods, but they work."

Her answer was a stiff nod. Not a good sign. The lady was cooperating for now, but he could already see the fight in her building. At some point, sooner rather than later he suspected, she was going to balk at his orders. No point borrowing trouble. He'd deal with the issue when it arose.

Unlocking the door, he urged her inside so he could disarm the security system. Closing the door behind him, he threw the deadbolt and entered another code that would alert him to any attempts to invade the property. Then he set the chimes on the doors, just in case she got fed up and tried to leave.

"Kitchen is straight ahead," he said. "You can check the supplies and let me know what to request so you're comfortable."

He dropped the bags. The last time he'd brought a client here, they'd been momentarily distracted from their troubles, in awe of the marble floors, gourmet kitchen, and fully stocked bar. Not to mention the sweeping view of the city. It wasn't the ocean, but even he approved.

When she continued to stand there, he headed to the kitchen. Eventually she'd follow. He opened the pantry door. "Take a look here and in the fridge," he said. "Anything you need or want can and will be delivered."

"I don't want food." She looked around the room, her eyes suspiciously bright. "I want justice and..." She turned away and shook her head.

"You want your life back," he said gently. "I'm afraid that's going to take more than a few hours." Mike indulged in another long study of the woman. She was beautiful and feisty. "Go choose a bedroom and make yourself at home. I'll handle the grocery list," he offered. Anything to get some distance. Petite in stature even with the high heels she'd slipped into at the motel, this spitfire blonde didn't lack an ounce in curve appeal, grit, or courage. He found the combination more tempting than he should.

"Is that another order?"

"If it needs to be." He'd just saved her from her own misguided attempt to help and from a killer, but she didn't seem impressed. "It may feel like we're sitting on our hands, but Claudia is gathering information we can use. We aren't going anywhere until we hear from her."

"Fine."

When she moved out of sight down the hallway, he took a deep breath, the first in a long while. He didn't worry about her sneaking out since every possible exit was wired. He'd be on her in seconds if she tried it. Unfortunately, it was all too easy to imagine how her sensual curves would feel under his hands. Not that she'd invite a normal guy like him to get that close. He could keep her alive, but he couldn't do a damn thing to advance her career. In this town that's what mattered most. Lauren Marie Woods hadn't reached the level of success she had achieved without making her career rather than her love life her priority.

He finished the grocery list and was just about to send it to Claudia when a text message came through from his assistant. He read it, enlarged the attached photo, and read the accompanying message twice more. "Damn."

Failure wasn't an option for the Guardian Agency. Miss Woods might just become the client that put a stain on their perfect record.

LAUREN TOSSED her purse and bag on the bed and flopped down between them. Yes, the safe house was gorgeous, but she didn't care about comfort. Desmond had been murdered, his life snuffed out while she watched in horror.

She needed to be out there *doing* something. Given the chance she'd shake Mike Stone until his teeth rattled. She needed someone to keep her safe *and* help her resolve the situation.

"He did save your life, Lauren," she muttered.

She rested her head in her hands. If it hadn't been for him, she would have walked right up to her car, clicked the unlock button as she reached for the door and been blown to bits. She groaned. What in the world was she going to do? News of Desmond's murder was everywhere. The latest announcement that she was a person of interest had likely gone viral by now. Her career was in jeopardy even if she survived the men trying to silence her.

Mike, cocky as he was, was right about the danger and the odds against her. More irritating was her strange inability to ignore that ripped body of his and handsome face. She worked with devastatingly handsome men every day. But his eyes... those striking blue eyes under dark, straight brows were a sharp contrast to his glossy black hair. Her body-guard was definitely leading man material—as long as the part didn't require him to be friendly.

She was being childish. To stay alive, she could tolerate his attitude. She had to. He'd proven the point that she needed him. Shivering, she got up and moved to the window to peer out over the city. She'd dealt with directors, producers, and even writers who'd been worse than Mike, but they'd never seized her phone or isolated her so effectively. This time the horrifying script was real life with real consequences.

Even more disconcerting, none of the directors, producers and writers with whom she had worked had ever made her wish for things she had no business even thinking about. The way her mind latched onto the details of Mike's handsome face or that incredibly hard body made her want to scream. Or moan. Yes, she understood the brain's natural tendency to find an escape hatch, but this was no time to indulge her long neglected libido.

Focus! She rubbed her hands on her hips, pacing the room. Detective Treadwell would think she was guilty when she didn't return his calls. Her friends would be worried about her. Was taking her phone a necessity or overkill? The image of her car exploding loomed in her mind. Those men who killed Desmond had known him, personally as well as professionally. The one had called her by name almost immediately after spotting her and somehow they had followed her to the motel. If she'd led them to a friend or to her hometown, the disaster would've multiplied.

No matter how she wanted to help, she wasn't equipped. She should be grateful to Mike Stone—no matter how pushy he was. Whatever business Desmond had been conducting, beyond his talent agency, had almost gotten her killed. She had no experience in dealing with that sort of trouble.

Lauren flopped back on the bed and stared up at the ceiling, pondering her options. Whenever she closed her eyes she saw that poor woman's face. Even now, in the quiet, secure bedroom of a safe house, that woman's screams echoed through Lauren's head.

She trembled against the awful memory. Was she still alive? Was she the eyewitness? If so, why didn't she just tell the truth? Lauren certainly wouldn't be a person of interest if she had.

Restless, she sat up and went through every detail, every sensation about last night once more. She couldn't remember seeing anyone else in the building. On the street, crowded with emergency vehicles and flashing lights, she had no idea who might have been watching. Lauren had been raised to be responsible and accountable. She wanted to go to the station and clear up the outrageous accusations. They couldn't possibly pin a homicide on her when she hadn't even been in the room.

Kicking off her heels, she stretched her toes and calves. When she got her phone back, she should find a lawyer. Neither of the lawyers with Desmond's agency would work. They weren't criminal specialists. She could reach out to a friend or two for a recommendation. The only good news was that the soap was finished shooting until after the holidays. If Mike helped her clear this up right away, the producers wouldn't have cause to fire her.

The idea that Christmas was swiftly approaching broadsided her. What a hell of a way to spend the days leading up to one of her favorite holidays. She'd been looking forward to spending her time off with friends. That wouldn't happen now. At this rate, she'd be lucky to still be alive on Christmas morning.

"No use feeling sorry for yourself." She hopped off the bed and decided to explore the house.

When she opened the door, Mike was there, hand raised to knock. "Join me in the office."

Another order. She swallowed the irritation. "Has something happened?"

"Claudia sent pictures for your review. I've got it set up in the office."

She braced for more bad news. "She found something?"

"Sooner than I expected, yes." He stepped back and guided her away from the bedroom.

Lauren had to avert her gaze as they strolled down the hallway. Maybe it was the tension, but she couldn't keep her eyes off his backside. The way he filled out those jeans was inspiring. Did he snap orders in bed? The errant thought startled her and she felt the heat creeping into her cheeks as he opened a door opposite the formal dining room. She really was *not* herself.

"Have a seat," he said, turning the desk chair for her.

She complied, leaning to the side as he reached around her and moved the mouse, bringing up a blue screen on the monitor. He was close enough that she caught the scent of soap on his skin and the lingering odor of the explosion in his hair.

What was wrong with her? She had a normal, healthy sex drive, even if it had been parked for a long time, but this was the worst time for it to kick into high gear. She hadn't felt a physical attraction to Desmond in years. On the occasions when she allowed herself to envision her future, when she thought of the ideal man she wanted in her life someday, she'd pictured someone far less polished and authoritarian than Desmond. Someone who listened and understood her, who saw through the public persona to the real woman she was underneath.

Something *must* be wrong, maybe even warped, to have her feeling such a sudden attraction to another I-know-what's-best-for-you man. In preparing for her role as Dr. Loveless, she'd consulted some top psychologists. When this mess was over she'd put in some couch time as a patient. She didn't want to repeat the mistakes she'd made with Desmond. She wanted a decent guy who didn't feel compelled to press opinions, expectations, and orders on her at every turn.

"Claudia pulled the crime scene photos," Mike warned, aiming the cursor at a folder on the screen. "Are you squeamish?"

"I saw it live and in color last night." The pictures couldn't be any worse than being there. Nothing could be as bad as the images of the murder that plagued her as she'd tried and failed to sleep last night.

Mike straightened. "Take it at your own pace then."

She opened the file and examined each picture, not bothering to ask how Claudia had acquired the evidence report so quickly. It took her a few minutes of clicking back and forth between angles to pinpoint the inconsistencies. Like Treadwell said, the woman's body wasn't in the room and there was no blood anywhere in the room except around Desmond.

She leaned forward, looking for anything the police might interpret in a way that made her look guilty. Paperwork had fallen from the desk, which didn't make sense to her as Desmond had a habit of keeping his desk clear.

"Wait." She used the mouse to enlarge one photo. Her blood turned cold when she recognized those papers as the script she'd been carrying. "That's wrong. I didn't go in." She couldn't catch her breath. "I wasn't in that room." She swiveled in the chair, her knees nearly knocking into Mike's legs.

"Are you referring to the script with the note on it?"

She nodded. "I dropped it in the hallway. Shock. They killed him and I dropped it. The sound alerted them and they chased me."

"You can see it's spattered with the victim's blood."

She saw it, but couldn't believe it. "I did *not* go into his office. I ran." She shook her head. "This doesn't make sense." She wanted to swear and yell and pound something or someone. "How? They set me up. I didn't go in. I swear. I never went in."

"I believe you, but the police can only work with what they find."

"They found *lies!*" She pushed back from the desk and stood but her knees had turned to jelly and she fell right back into the chair.

"Take it easy, Lauren. We'll figure this out."

She minimized the file, unable to bear the sight of the accusing pictures. "How could they have known I would be there to play the part of their scapegoat?"

"They didn't," Mike said with jarring confidence. "They expected to get away with it. Would have, but you interrupted. They will get away with it if they can make you a believable patsy."

"And kill me before the truth comes out." Her thoughts twisted and tangled as she tried to make sense of this terrible mess. "The woman. We have to find her. She knows the truth."

Mike leaned his hip against the desk. "Whether she'll tell the truth is another matter."

Lauren turned her face up to his. "What do you mean?"

"Worst case scenario?"

She nodded.

"The fact that she isn't dead in the office suggests that she was in on it with the two men you saw."

A chill skated over her skin. Desmond had been fooled more than once by a gorgeous face. She closed her eyes, trying to remember where she'd seen that woman. "What's the best case scenario?"

He scowled at the monitor. "Unfortunately, I can't see one yet."

"We have to find her. And talk to her." Lauren closed her eyes, determined to figure it out. Where had she seen that woman? The image of a bar… then the woman's face. "Wait." She replayed the images again. "She works in a bar, I think. Maybe she's a bartender or a waitress." Her thoughts immediately turned to the long list of Desmond's favorite clubs.

"I'll put Claudia on the search for LA bartenders and waitresses who match your description but you need to keep your expectations real. The task will be like looking for a needle in a haystack."

"How real?"

"The criminals think you're a threat. The police think you're a suspect. The woman is only a wild-card. You don't know what Desmond was involved in." He ticked each point off on his fingers. "You need to stay here, out of sight, until we figure this out. It could take some time."

"There has to be another way." She shook her head and forced herself to stand. This time, she managed it without swaying. "I have professional obligations."

"Your show isn't shooting right now."

"An acting career isn't that simple." She'd never been a passive person. A small voice in her head reminded her she'd been way too passive about Desmond. "There's a community event I'm supposed to attend tomorrow. An interview next week. I can't just skip those. Someone has to plan Desmond's funeral. He has no other... family."

Mike folded his arms, staring down at her. "First, Trinity's body won't be released for a while so no rush on a funeral. Second, a public appearance is out of the question. Besides, no one expects you to carry on as usual right now. Your lover was murdered. You're grieving."

She wanted to argue with him, but he was right. Instead, she started to pace the room as another approach popped like a light bulb in her mind. "A public appearance might be exactly what we need. I can draw the bad guys out. It's a classic strategy."

"Absolutely not."

What else could she do? "I know Desmond's passwords," she said. "If we go by the office maybe we can figure out what he was doing for those men."

"Not today." He shook his head, his eyes tracking her movements like some kind of predatory cat. "Your car just blew up. You're a person of interest in a murder case. People will see you in every petite blonde in the city. And let's not forget the Trinity office is a crime scene. His computer has probably already been seized as evidence. I'll confirm that with Claudia. The police will have the office as well as the house under surveillance looking for you."

"If we wait, the woman could disappear... or end up dead."

"True," he said. "But everyone is hunting for you. Too much risk."

She rubbed her hands up and down her chilled arms. She had to find something plausible he couldn't argue with. "If the woman wasn't with Desmond by chance, maybe she was the distraction that allowed them to catch Desmond at an inopportune time."

"Maybe."

"You're not going to go with any of my suggestions, got it." Lauren stalked out of the office. Faced with the kitchen and bar, the marvelous view, or sulking in the bedroom, she opted for the bar. It was far too early, but she poured vodka into a glass and added just enough cranberry juice to give it some color. The first sip burned away the frayed edges of her nerves and shushed the scared voice in her head threatening to erupt into uncontrolled panic.

What in the hell was Desmond into? Why that woman? Angry all over again, Lauren went to the kitchen and dumped the remainder of her drink down the drain. Being fuzzy-headed was the last thing she needed. Her stomach rumbled, reminding her she hadn't eaten since late yesterday. If they weren't going anywhere, she could make herself useful and prepare lunch. Doing anything was better than doing nothing.

How could she have known Desmond Trinity so

intimately for all those years and not have recognized he was far more than a top-notch agent and so much worse than a perpetual cheater? How long had he been involved with those men? She had never seen either of them at any of the parties they hosted or attended. She'd never heard the names Nikoli or Andreas before. Although Hollywood seemed like a big city, the television and film community was actually fairly small. Almost everyone knew everyone else.

Had she been so successful in building that wall between her and Desmond that she ignored the trouble he'd gotten himself into? The thought made her inexplicably sad.

Whatever happened to all those dreams she'd had of love and happily ever after as a young girl? In these days of uncoupling and overnight divorces, maybe true love no longer existed. She thought of the man in the other room and how he'd saved her. In a movie he would be her knight in shining armor. He would defend her honor and they'd ride off into the sunset together.

Only this was real life and knights in shining armor didn't exist anymore.

CHAPTER 4

MIKE SCRUBBED AT HIS FACE. His eyes were dry. He and Claudia had been at this for hours without making any progress on identifying the woman Lauren had seen in Trinity's office. Claudia had confirmed that the witness and the woman Lauren saw were one and the same but the cops had not released her name.

"Looks like the only way to learn what Trinity was doing is by shaking the bushes," Claudia said. "If you allow Miss Woods to reach out to her sources, you might just get lucky."

And there was the catch. He couldn't let her reach out *and* ensure her safety. "Based on Lauren's account, I'm thinking these guys are Russian mafia. If I'm right, they should be in at least one of the databases we've accessed." The cops as well as the FBI and other federal and international agencies typically had significant info on the mob types, but nothing along those lines had been mentioned in press releases.

"They'd have to be powerfully connected for someone to be keeping them off the grid like this," Claudia murmured.

"Have you got any contacts you can reach out to?" Mike needed intel. He couldn't help Lauren without it.

"One or two. I'll get back to you."

"I'll be standing by."

The call ended and Mike swiveled in the chair. Facing the door, he debated several less than ideal options. Lauren got under his skin in ways he couldn't quite define. Part of it was her skill as an actress. He'd always been damned good at reading people, but with her not so much. How was he supposed to know what was real and what was just for show when she could turn it off and on instantly?

He'd sent a text to Hank, asking if Sadie knew Lauren personally or by reputation, but the women had never crossed paths. Mike was tired of dead ends today.

She claimed the missing woman was familiar in the same breath she claimed no knowledge of her boyfriend's illegal activities. The two factors just didn't add up. Claudia had found the individual bank accounts for Trinity and Lauren. The two had kept their finances completely independent of each other. That allowed for some of Lauren's ignorance of Trinity's activities, but certainly not all. She'd lived with him and worked closely with him for years.

Mike glanced at his watch. She'd offered to make a sandwich for him hours ago. He'd declined but his appetite was suddenly revving into high gear. He headed for the kitchen, the scents drifting out to meet him making his stomach growl. "Did you get bored?"

She glanced up from the pot she was stirring. She'd twisted her long blond hair up and out of the way, but little wisps were curling in the fragrant steam rising from whatever she had going on the stove top. "We have to eat." She shrugged. "There wasn't any bread for sandwiches."

His stomach rumbled again. "What's on the menu?"

"Red sauce and pasta." She made a face. "There wasn't a lot to choose from. Do you want a beer or something stronger to go with it? There seems to be a good supply of alcohol."

He laughed. "Water." He wouldn't risk the alcohol dulling his reflexes while on the job.

As he watched, she moved through the kitchen, a picture of domestic grace that gave him a strange sense that he'd been missing something like this in his life. She filled two glasses with water and piled pasta high on a plate. She added the sauce and a scoop of steamed broccoli before passing the plate to him.

"You didn't have to go to all this trouble," he said, shaking off the momentary daze.

"No trouble," she answered with a small shrug. "It gave me something to do."

She made a smaller plate for herself and sat at the other end of the kitchen island. For several minutes he ate, wondering how she'd tweaked the sauce. It never tasted this good when he poured it straight from the jar. He pointed with his fork. "What'd you do to this?"

"Just added a bit of this and that for a kick," she said.

"It's good."

She smiled. "Thank you."

They ate in silence for a while. Then he asked, "You and Trinity kept separate bank accounts."

"I insisted on it."

"Why?"

She sighed. Her gaze didn't stray from her pasta. "At the beginning of our relationship it was too good to be true. Girl from Kansas finds her Oz, you know? Every day I was sure he'd wake up and be done with me so I didn't want to take a chance on joint bank accounts. As my agent, my paychecks went through him anyway. He took his cut and I got the rest. I didn't think he needed to know what I did with my money."

"From what Claudia found, you've been smart with your money." He'd been surprised by just how smart. Anyone who thought there weren't any brains behind all that beauty would be dead wrong.

Lauren nodded, and then sipped her water. "I grew up poor. Being poor in Kansas is one thing, being poor here is another. I made up my mind early on to save and invest a hefty chunk of my earnings. I sent some back home for my mom, supported a few charities, and live comfortably on the rest." She tipped her head, gracing him with a direct look. "In light of recent events, it seems my precautions were prudent."

Crap. She didn't realize how stuck she was. "You can't access any of it," he said. "The police will be keeping an eye out for any financial activity. This witness might even give them a reason to freeze your accounts."

She set her fork aside. "Which adds yet another layer of urgency to my predicament."

"Lauren." He'd wanted to get her talking, not worry her. "Anything you need, I'll take care of it. Money is not an issue for you right now."

"Thanks. It sounds like I need to find something that connects Desmond to the killers." She set her fork aside. "If the police stop looking for suspects, I may never be able to prove what really happened."

"When was the last time you caught Trinity with another woman?"

She slowly looked up and met his gaze. "Why does that matter?"

"I'm trying to get a handle on the man." *And you.* She insisted on making it clear that Trinity was currently only her agent, not her boyfriend, but the two had been cohabitating for years.

"I did my best not to catch him." She patted those lush lips with her napkin.

"By avoiding the office?"

"At all costs," she said quietly, pushing her plate away. "He was smart enough not to bring other women home."

Mike felt a surge of anger over what Trinity had put her through. What she'd allowed the jerk to put her through. "But you knew when he was involved elsewhere."

"Yes." She sat stiffly, her hands in her lap. "Two years ago I caught him at the office after hours. It was the only time I saw him in the act of seducing a potential client. He called it business. I called it cheating. We eventually came to an agreement that I wouldn't leave him and he'd be more discreet about his extracurricular activities."

"But you went up to the office after hours last night."

"Last night, that script…" She rolled her eyes. "It was the last straw for me and long past time to cut ties as his client and as his roommate—separate bedrooms, for the past two years, in case you're wondering." She got up and carried her plate to the sink.

Mike couldn't imagine a relationship riddled with infidelity. He detested emotional games and liars even more. Why did anyone put up with that? A woman with Lauren's fire, beauty, and talent should've left at the first sign of trouble. But she'd stayed. For the sake of her career. Jesus, Hollywood was twisted. "What happened to her?"

"Who?" Lauren asked, leaning back against the counter as she dried her hands on the towel.

"The woman you caught him with two years ago." Mike wished like hell the man was still alive so he could beat him senseless.

"I don't know. I've made it a point not to think about that, but my guess is he either chose not to represent her or she never made the cut with any studio."

"But you have that memory for faces and detail," he said, with complete sincerity. "Would you recognize her again if you saw her?"

Lauren caught her full lower lip between her teeth. "Probably."

His instincts were sparking. This was bigger than Lauren getting caught in the wrong place at the wrong time by a pair of lethal men. "So, the fact is, she didn't make it big or you would have run into her somewhere."

She nodded. "I suppose that's true."

"How many clients did Trinity represent?"

"It varied from year to year. He was the agent

everyone wanted. His ability to identify and match talent with the right roles was unprecedented. Why?"

"Just thinking." About the dead talent agent and the mysterious witness who'd contradicted Lauren's account of the murder. "Did Trinity ever travel out of the country?"

"Once or twice a year, but I didn't go with him."

"Because?" He'd bet good money Trinity made his travel plans to purposely exclude her.

She made a small production of replacing the hand towel on the rack. "The dates conflicted with my schedule on the set of Harper Cove."

"So your relationship with Trinity really was just for show." It wasn't a question. The answer was clear to him now. For whatever reason, Trinity had liked or needed the image of stability with Lauren. Was she an unwitting part of his cover?

"Maybe not at first, but in recent years, yes." The admission cost her. The pain in her eyes gave away just how much.

He almost wished he could take back the question. But if her feelings were the only thing that got hurt before they figured this out, he would be damned happy about it and call the case a success. The idea that she'd gotten out of that building alive still stunned him.

Assuming the killers had watched her and tailed her from the crime scene to the police station and then to her motel, why not just kill her? They obviously wanted her dead and there would've been ample opportunities before she'd reached the motel and after. Instead, they'd staged the crime scene to implicate her and then wired a bomb into her car. Why the extra step?

"What's going through your head?" she asked, returning to the island and her chair.

Too many things and he was only ready to share one of them. "We need to determine if the police on this case can be trusted."

Her eyes lit up. "I'd very much like the answer to that question."

He wasn't sure she fully understood the danger involved in finding out. "What I have in mind might not work at all," he warned. In fact, his idea could backfire in stunning fashion.

"If there's any chance, I want to try," she replied.

His job was to protect her. End of story. If Claudia confirmed his worst suspicions, Lauren would never be safe unless the men who'd murdered Trinity were behind bars. "We'll set up a meet for first thing tomorrow. Until then, relax and try to get some rest."

To his surprise, she didn't argue. He didn't know her industry as well as she did, but he knew human nature. Her ex was into something serious and Mike wanted to know if it had started before or after Lauren had come to Hollywood with stars in her eyes. More importantly, he wanted to know if Trinity had somehow been using her for some agenda she couldn't see.

Mike worked for hours brainstorming and fine-tuning the specifics until he'd worked out a plan Claudia could support. When they had the details set, he returned to the living room to talk it through and found Lauren curled into a corner of the couch sound asleep. The television volume was no more than a soft murmur. She'd chosen an old romantic movie. The stress had caught up with her and he hated to wake her. Her body relaxed, she looked fresh and tempting from her hands tucked under her chin all the way to the pale pink polish on her toes.

Watching her, he felt something long-dormant stir deep inside his gut. The need to protect her, to keep her from harm was part of it. That was the job. Desire sizzled through his blood, but he ignored it. What man wouldn't be attracted to that exceptional package? She was far more than the gorgeous exterior. She was smart and witty and caring.

He grabbed a throw from the back of the loveseat and draped it over her, careful not to touch her or linger over the process. Weighing the options, he stretched out on the floor to watch the end of the movie. Staying in here with her was expedient. He'd know the minute she woke up and he could go over his plan right away. He even believed the tale as he dozed off to the barely audible bar fight playing out on the television.

THURSDAY, *December 11, 10:30 a.m.*

Mike backed into an open space near the parking garage exit. He turned off the car and handed Lauren a ball cap to hide her hair. It probably wasn't the right accessory for her snug jeans, tunic, and the rose-colored winter sweater, but that was the point. They didn't want her to be recognized.

Jeans and a half-zip sweatshirt over a black tee was enough of a disguise for him. He had a gun in his waistband at the small of his back and another at his ankle, plus his knife just in case things turned ugly. Hopefully none of that would be necessary.

The decoy the agency had hired to impersonate Lauren would enter the building across the street in just fifteen minutes. The police had been tipped off that Lauren was meeting with an attorney to discuss turning herself in. This building, the one he and Lauren were about to enter, was still under construction. Claudia had made arrangements for them to access the sixth floor where they would wait to see who showed up for the party.

"Ready?" Mike studied Lauren's perfect profile.

She nodded, donning dark sunglasses.

"Do you want to talk through it one more time?"

"We go in quietly. Ignore anyone we encounter inside." She paused to gulp in some air. "We take the stairs to the sixth floor and then we watch." Her lips stretched into a smile but he didn't miss the slight tremble in the expression. "It's just like blocking a scene."

He'd have to take her word on that. Leaving the car was a big risk, despite the precautions. They'd discussed pros, cons, and fallback strategy over breakfast. She'd embraced all of it with enthusiasm. She understood the importance of this first step. Since a decoy was in place, they could have stayed at the safe house, but Lauren's ability to recognize faces was needed. Her job was to look for anyone in the area that she might have seen with Trinity.

Walking beside her, Mike kept his eyes open wide and his senses on point. He'd chosen a congested area smack in the middle of LA's infamous Box. From eight to five, the Box was the city's hectic business district. After five, however, all bets were off. The shops closed for the day and trouble seemed to ooze from every crack in the sidewalks.

"Are you nervous?" he asked as they entered the newest high rise on the block. He'd been in similar situations with clients. Here with Lauren it all felt new to him and the burst of nerves was disconcerting.

"A little," she said, pulling the ball cap low. "What if one of the workers recognizes me?"

"I've got it all covered," he said. "Just brave it out with me." He suppressed a grin when her chin came up and she stood a little taller.

No one from the construction crew paid the slightest attention to their entrance. They walked in as if they owned the place. Everything went according to plan as they climbed the stairs. Once they took their positions at a towering window overlooking the street and the building the decoy would enter, Lauren removed the high-powered binoculars Mike had tucked in her purse.

"Maybe I'll write a screen play about an actress who witnesses her agent being murdered by a mob guy." She lifted the binoculars to her eyes. "Should be a blockbuster."

Mike chuckled. He was glad to see her a little more relaxed. Yesterday had been tough for her. He liked that more of the fear had been replaced by determination. The same tenacity that had made her a success in this business was what she needed to get through the nightmare that had descended on her life.

"Take your time," he said, "study each face you see."

"Okay." Her teeth dug into that plump lower lip.

Rather than stand there and wish it were him toying with that sexy lip, he withdrew a compact set of binoculars from his back pocket and surveyed the vehicles parked along the street below.

"So the working theory is if the bad guys show up," she said, focused on the street below, "we'll know someone in the police department is feeding them information."

"Since Treadwell is the only person you contacted about the meeting that would be a definite yes."

She lowered her glasses and turned to him. "Maybe I'm more naïve than I thought, but I'm hoping Treadwell is one of the good guys."

The words had barely left her lips when Mike spotted a black SUV easing to the curb at the end of the block. He zeroed in on the driver. It was the man Lauren believed to be named Nikoli. Mike sent a text to Claudia so the decoy could be alerted. When she exited the building, she would no longer look anything like Lauren Marie Woods.

"Oh, God." Lauren sagged. "They're here."

She swayed a little and he steadied her. Crazy as it was, he wished he could have sheltered her from yet another let down.

LONG MINUTES LATER, Lauren felt sick as they moved swiftly down the six flights of stairs. Why would Detective Treadwell sell her out to the killers? Officer Cooper thought the detective was good at his job. Did Treadwell have everyone fooled?

Her thoughts in a whirl, she registered Mike ushering her into his Camaro, his hand warm and strong at her back. When they'd driven away, she was thankful he was keeping an eye out for trouble. She was too deep in the haze of disbelief.

"What made you decide to take the part as Dr. Loveless?"

Lauren almost gave herself whiplash turning to look at him. "Excuse me?"

He kept his eyes on the street, navigating the traffic. "I've heard a lot of actors think daytime soaps are beneath them. What made you take the job?"

She stared at the view through the windshield, unable to concentrate. The colorful lights draped on shop windows reminded her that Christmas was only a couple of weeks away. She'd put up the tree and decorated it over the weekend. Desmond hadn't seemed to notice. He never did. Christmas was nothing more than an excuse to have big parties to him. Since her mom died, there was no reason for her to go home for the holidays so she'd made her time off from work about the parties as well and spending time with friends.

Not anymore. Desmond was dead and the police were doing nothing to catch his killer. No matter that the romantic side of the relationship was long over, she felt suddenly alone.

"Was it the steady pay?"

She blinked away the blur of tears, drawing herself back to the moment and away from the painful thoughts. Why was her bodyguard so persistent? "When I was a kid, my mom watched one show every day. Religiously. She said that no matter what else was going on it gave her an hour of escape. So, yes, it was the regular paycheck but it was also the hope that I would give fans like my mom the same escape-entertainment she enjoyed. It's good for the soul."

"Really?" His grin flashed. "Is that according to Lauren Marie Woods or Dr. Loveless? What about those of us who prefer other ways to escape?"

"To each his own," she said. "I'm sure you wouldn't choose a daytime drama as an escape any more than I'd choose a firing range."

"A firing range is a fun way to kill a couple of hours."

"The only thing I ever got from a firing range was a sore shoulder and a headache."

"Wait a second," he gave her a long look while they waited for a traffic light to change. "When were you been on a firing range?"

"Growing up in Kansas involved plenty of target practice starting with a .22 rifle. I learned how to carry and fire a Glock 9 millimeter for my second movie. Directors are all about making a character believable for the audience. I've studied psychology relentlessly for my role on Harper Cove."

He shifted in his seat and checked the mirrors. "You think the audience really believes you know anything about being a psychologist?"

"I hope they do. Anything less would ruin their experience with Harper Cove."

He shook his head. "That's pretty sad."

Once again, his dismissive attitude about actors annoyed her. She crossed her arms over her chest. "What bothers you more, that I get paid to pretend to be someone else or that people like me?"

"Neither."

"You are so full of crap," she replied.

"Is that a professional assessment, doctor?"

"Call it a friendly diagnosis from a girl with daddy issues," she snapped.

He pulled into the driveway and hit the button to raise the garage door. "Your old man doesn't approve of your career choice?" he asked as he cut the engine.

She held his gaze, wondering why she felt compelled to answer such a personal question. "He does not. He also didn't approve of the way I slipped out from under his thumb and dropped out of college." She released her seatbelt and climbed out of the car. "I paid him back for the tuition costs, with interest, but some people cut ties forever." She rolled her shoulders, mentally dropping the weight of her past. "I haven't seen him since my mom died."

"I guess we have something in common." He closed his door and hit lock.

"Your mom died?"

He shook his head. "The dad part. Mine's a judgmental, unforgiving—"

"But you still love him anyway," Lauren interrupted.

Mike stared at her for a long moment before answering. "Something like that." He unlocked the door and disarmed the security system. "Claudia should have suspect photos ready for you by now," he said as they walked inside and he reset the system.

"Great." No reason to be scared of mug shots. "And after that?" Inside the house, she didn't need the thick cardigan sweater anymore, but she snuggled into it for comfort.

"One step at a time."

It wasn't exactly the answer she'd wanted to hear but at least it was progress. They were moving forward and that was the only way to reach the end of this nightmare.

CHAPTER 5

WHILE LAUREN PREPARED LUNCH, Mike dove into the reports Claudia had compiled. The news was disturbing and he wasn't looking forward to briefing Lauren. Rather than ruin her appetite, he returned to the kitchen to make sure she ate something first. The pantry and fridge had been stocked while they were out so Lauren had filled two big bowls of salad. He normally wasn't big on rabbit food, but he had to admit the berries and nuts gave this one just the right crunch and plenty of flavor. After they'd cleaned up, he had no choice but to give her the bad news.

He brought his laptop to the kitchen island. "Have a seat."

When she'd settled on a stool, he chose the one next to her. He ignored the way his body reacted to her nearness. She'd gotten into his head like no other woman. He wanted to believe she knew the right keywords from her psych research, but after learning they shared a history of disappointed fathers he feared it was less guesswork and more genuine connection. The thought wasn't comforting in the least. Business first, everything else was secondary.

He opted to start with the photos Claudia had sent. "Take your time and let me know if any of these people are familiar," he instructed as he opened the laptop.

Lauren tipped her head, eyeing him over her cup of tea. "You had Claudia pull these based on the sketches."

He nodded. "I've been looking into local organized crime since your car exploded. That's the usual approach when they want to make a big statement." He was also wondering why the police hadn't asked her to look at similar photos the night of the murder.

She looked up at him, her eyes wide with renewed worry. "You think they're planning to make an example of me?"

"Not you. Trinity. The hit may have been a warning to the others in their supply chain."

"But we still don't know what product Desmond supplied."

He shrugged. "I have a few thoughts on that. Only time and more work will prove me right or wrong." Russian syndicates were in a constant state of motion, ruthlessly developing territories and interests that increased the cash flow. Before she could ask him about his thoughts, he went to the fridge for a cola. He didn't want to distract her or to create any doubt about the veracity of her identifications when she made them.

A few minutes later, she looked up, her eyes wide. "I found the guy who shot Desmond." When he sat down beside her, she pointed to the monitor. "This is the man. Nikoli."

"You're sure?" Mike asked. Her finger was aimed at a mug shot of a Krushka syndicate enforcer named Nikoli Maksimov.

She glared daggers at the screen, but the fear showed in the way she swallowed before she answered him. "This man hit Desmond according to the orders given, and then he shot him. Twice. The boss called him Nikoli."

"All right." Mike nodded. "Take a breath. You're doing great. See if the other guy is in that mix."

He pushed back his chair, needing the distance while she looked at more pictures. Suddenly she turned her back on the screen. Her face had gone pale and her hands trembled in her lap. "That's him. He gave the orders. When I ran, he made me a hideous offer, but when I pulled the fire alarm he said he'd kill me."

Mike fought off the urge to comfort her. "Show me."

She shifted so he could see a picture of Peter Kozlov. Mike closed the laptop. If she struggled this much over the faces, she'd have a break down at the sight of the rap sheets. She'd had a rough enough time watching through those binoculars today. As disappointed as he'd been when those two thugs showed up today, what absolutely twisted his gut was the idea that Treadwell had tipped off the Russians. He was the only person Lauren called. Equally telling was the lack of media coverage. Beyond passing the information along to Kozlov, Treadwell had apparently pretended Lauren hadn't made the call. All of which confirmed they could *not* go to the police at this time. There was no way to know for sure who they could trust. Mike wasn't taking that kind of chance with her life.

He walked around the island and leaned against it, using the expanse of granite to keep his hands to himself. He'd never wanted to comfort a woman more.

When she looked up, her eyes so sad, he knew the four feet of polished rock wouldn't hold him back for long. "Who are they?"

"Russian mob. Specifically the Krushka syndicate."

She pressed her fingers to her lips for a moment. "Desmond was a talent agent. What business would they have with him?"

"You heard them talk about a product."

"Yes, but I have no idea what they meant."

"Based on what I know about these men, Kozlov

in particular, going back out in public again before we resolve this would be far riskier than we suspected."

"But we have names. Can't you just take me to the police now?"

"Not if you want to live. We have names, but no evidence. There's a big difference and don't forget, Treadwell, or someone he told," Mike hedged, "tipped these guys off about your meeting with the lawyer."

She squeezed her hands more tightly. "What about the FBI?"

"Before we go to any branch of law enforcement," he explained, "we need evidence to back up our accusations. Once we break cover and take that step, there's no going back, Lauren. We have to do this right. It's the only way I can protect you."

Her gaze drifted back to the laptop. "These people are that bad, huh?"

He'd always believed delivering bad news was like ripping off a bandage. Do it fast and quick. No point changing that strategy now. "Kozlov worked his way up through the syndicate, earning his current post here. He has a hand in prostitution, the drug trade, and is suspected of money laundering, car theft, and worse. Nothing sticks."

"He's the boss now?"

"According to the information Claudia dug up, he seems to be the top dog locally. No one's made a play on his territories in over a year. He has informants everywhere. I'm sure he has more than one cop on his payroll and if you went to the police, he'd have you killed before you could do much more than state your name."

She closed her eyes for a moment. "You're saying there's nothing we can do?" When she opened her eyes once more, they glistened and he thought she might start crying, but no tears fell.

"We'll see. No promises. Let's talk about that night again. What exactly did Kozlov say to you?"

"He said he knew how to take care of a beautiful woman. That he'd put the world at my feet and that he was more powerful than... Desmond." Her brows pleated into a frown. "What are you thinking?"

This was the part he dreaded telling her the most. Mike had a bad feeling about the product Trinity had been providing. "Peter Kozlov has known associates in human trafficking as well as prostitution."

"What?" She lurched to her feet and began to pace. "Desmond wouldn't be a part of anything like that." She spread her hands, palms up. "What use did he have for prostitutes when an endless parade of young women eager to audition by casting couch marched right up to him?"

"But aren't escorts a fairly common thing in your circles?" He'd tried to frame it nicely, but he could tell by the flicker of fire in her eyes he'd failed.

"Not *my* circles," she stated. "I'm aware it happens, but paying for sex just wasn't Desmond's style. As I said, plenty of women threw themselves at him free of charge."

Back to the direct method. "Lauren, based on what you saw, Kozlov knew Trinity. He knew you. That says he's familiar with Trinity on a personal level as well as a professional one. A man with Kozlov's reputation wouldn't do a face-to-face meeting if there wasn't something big on the line."

She stopped pacing mid-path and rubbed her temples. "I don't understand why Desmond would take such a risk with his reputation. He makes—made—a fortune as a talent agent. Why would he need to do something like this?"

"For some, there's never enough money, power, or influence. Any ideas how Trinity met Kozlov?"

"No." She shook her head, worry etched across her forehead. "We basically led separate lives under the same roof for the past two years." She started pacing again. "It has to be drugs. Desmond didn't use, but he would arrange things for some clients." She made a sound of frustration. "I guess it's possible he went to that extreme."

Mike stifled a sigh and went back for the laptop. "Let's follow that thread." He pulled up a file of perps tied to the Russian drug trade, with a few of the prostitutes thrown in. "Recognize anyone?"

She didn't. He opened another file. Knowing what was coming, he fought to soften the blow. "How about any of these faces?"

Dutifully, she looked at the screen and then frowned. "These aren't mug shots."

"Just click the box if the person in the photo seems familiar."

She clicked three, scrolled some more and clicked another. "Four so far. Who are they?"

"All of those women are listed as missing."

"Since when?"

"Six months ago to three years back. None of them are from California. Why were they familiar to you?"

"Occasionally Desmond brought home head shots and resumes of clients he was considering. I recognize three of them from the headshots. The fourth woman I saw at the office on one of my rare visits."

"Do you recall anything else?"

"I really tried to stay out of his way." She shook her head. "You must think I'm the biggest idiot for letting him cheat on me and dictate the terms of my career and personal life."

"I'm not here to judge you. I'm here to keep you out of the line of fire."

She turned and walked away.

"Where are you going?"

"I need to move." She stopped at the door. "I need to do something." She pushed her hands through her hair. "This is unthinkable. What you're suggesting…" She pressed her lips tight for a moment. "I couldn't have been this blind."

"You can't leave the house." Not until there was a hell of a good reason to take that kind of risk.

"I got that part loud and clear. There's an exercise room. I need to burn through this helpless feeling."

Mike let her go. She'd hit her limit. It wasn't a big leap, but it was progress, tying Trinity to several pretty, young, and now-missing women. He emailed the names back to Claudia. Mike feared any nice memories Lauren had of her former agent and lover were about to be obliterated. Somehow, he felt really bad about being the one showing her that ugly truth.

Lauren was bold and smart. She didn't fit his image of a spoiled actress and she was damned talented. His old nightmares had roused him last night and he'd decided to watch a few episodes of Harper Cove. He was damned glad she hadn't caught him.

He wished like hell he could get an accurate read on her. Too often he found himself wondering if he was looking at the actress or the real woman. Maybe he was better off not knowing which was which.

LAUREN STARTED ON THE TREADMILL, getting her blood pumping while she watched breaking news headlines trail across the bottom of the muted television screen. The home she'd shared with Desmond was surrounded by news crews. The police hadn't released anything else about her. Paparazzi were claiming sightings of her all over town. She even caught a glimpse of that damned black SUV in one of the aerial views.

"Bastards," she growled.

"That's probably undermining the good endorphin thing," Mike said, walking in.

He wore a dark t-shirt and loose gym shorts and if she hadn't already been warm and sweaty from the workout, she'd be spiking a fever about now. The man took hot and tempting to an all new level. "You'd rather have music?"

"Doesn't matter to me. I stop listening once I'm in the zone."

"Okay." She struggled to keep her running rhythm. "I keep watching, hoping to see something about the witness."

"And have you?"

"No." The treadmill hummed as the incline increased with the program she'd chosen. Her quads burned and she embraced it as affirmation of being alive.

Across the room at the multi-function machine, Mike set his weight load and then positioned himself for the bench press. Catching herself sneaking glances at him, enamored by the bunch and flex of his arms, she had to make a concentrated effort to return her gaze to the television.

"Sometimes it's easier if you stop thinking about it," he said.

"Huh?" Could he tell she was practically drooling over his body? Somewhere in the back of her mind she understood this instant attraction was a defense mechanism—a way to escape the awful reality of her life right now. Good grief, couldn't she think of a better way than ogling her protector?

"The woman from the office."

Thank heaven he assumed her mind was on the case. "I don't understand why she would have told the police a different story, but it's not just her. I keep trying to figure out what I missed." She would figure this out. Desmond might have kept her in the dark, but she didn't have to stay there. She had been right there in his life while he helped the Russian mob. She felt an obligation to help uncover his crimes and see justice done.

It was apparently arm day for Mike, because he moved to triceps dips while she entered her cool down phase on the treadmill. She doubled her efforts not to stare at him. The man really was… gorgeous. Stifling a groan, she forced her attention back on the screen just as her face popped up in upper right hand corner. She watched as the same bulletin was repeated about her being wanted for questioning, blah, blah, blah. Frustrated, she turned it off.

"Do you want music?" The quiet she'd enjoyed

when she'd been in here alone seemed too loud now that he'd joined her.

"You already asked me," Mike replied. "Just find something if you need it."

She blotted the sweat from her neck as she tuned the radio to a pop station and turned it up just enough to block the sound of his breathing. "This place is nicely equipped," she said, moving to the Pilates reformer. She felt his gaze on her as she began the first of a leg series and felt marginally better she wasn't the only one ogling today.

"Yep," he agreed, shifting his gaze away from her.

"I always feel like a ballerina when—" She froze mid-motion, her leg in the middle of a full arc. "That's it." She sat up as quickly as possible, freeing her foot from the strap. "The woman from the office was a ballerina. Sort of. Vanya... Vanya Something. Desmond probably never told me her last name."

Mike gave up on his triceps and walked over to sit next to her. "What else?"

"I accused him of cheating again when he told me he was working with her as a teacher."

"He wanted to study ballet?"

"Not quite." She shook her head, remembering the conversation. "No, he wanted her to teach some of his new clients. He gave me some line about starting a finishing school for prospective clients with the right look but too many rough edges."

"Where did this Vanya person teach?"

"I have no idea. I never gave it another thought. To me, it was just Desmond finding another way to cheat on me with clients dumb enough to fall for his lines the way I did. He never mentioned it again."

"You're not dumb."

His immediate defense surprised her. "Please." She blotted the sweat from her neck. "All this happened right under my nose. I should've noticed something before the bullets started flying."

"Thinking the best of someone isn't a crime. We all make mistakes, the key is learning from them. From where I'm sitting you're a quick learner."

"Thanks." She realized he was sitting very close to her. Her body yearned to be closer still. Not smart to latch onto the man trying to help her, no matter how much he intrigued her. It wasn't fair to either of them.

As if he'd suddenly read her mind, he stood. "I'm glad you remembered more about her."

"Will it help?" she asked, appreciating the view of his broad shoulders tapering to trim hips and powerful legs. A swimmer's build, she thought, which made perfect sense since he'd been a Navy SEAL.

"It's progress. I need to get this information to Claudia."

She sighed as he walked away, alone again with thoughts ricocheting like a pinball between her predicament and the sexy hunk assigned to help her get out of it. She finished her workout and took a shower, only to have him knocking at the bathroom door the minute she turned off the water.

"It's urgent," he said. "Meet me in the office."

"Fine." She hurried, hopeful that this time he had good news. She refused to consider that it could be worse. "No borrowing trouble," she grumbled to herself.

Dressed and emotionally braced for anything, she knocked on the open office door. "I'm here."

He was still in workout gear as he popped out of the chair. "Claudia found an informant willing to give us a lead. Apparently, Trinity was eye-ball deep into human trafficking."

Her stomach dropped. She'd known Desmond couldn't be innocent, but complicit? "What do you mean?"

"Your boyfriend—"

"Agent."

"Yeah, yeah." He frowned at her. "This is really ugly, Lauren."

"What's worse than unwittingly associating with a man who buys and sells people?"

"Fair point." Mike turned his laptop so she could see the screen. "Meet Andreas Polzin. He lives like a Russian Czar off the revenue from dozens of illegal enterprises run by highly competent, brutal criminal lieutenants like Kozlov."

The man in the photo was classically handsome,

but his dark eyes were cold, devoid of any emotion. Lauren's body started to quake. "I need a drink."

"You'll need more than that." Mike took a deep breath and let it out slowly. "Vanya connects all the players. You saw her with Trinity that night, which means she must have left the scene with Kozlov and his pal Maksimov. Word is, she's Polzin's California mistress." Mike sat down again and started typing. "I'll need Claudia's help to finish this."

"Finish what? Please spell it out! Not all of us are familiar with Russian crime." There was a clear excitement in his eyes, but it wasn't a happy or pleasant expression. There was something underneath, something predatory. It added a chill to the tremors. Dear God... what had she ignored all these years?

"Sit down before you faint."

"I will not faint." But she landed hard in the nearest chair. "Just tell me what the hell this all means."

He grunted. "Bottom line, we need to deal with Kozlov so you can have a life again."

"We need to deal with him so he goes down for the horrific crimes he's committed," she said. There were bigger issues than restoring the life she'd enjoyed twenty-four hours ago. These monstrous men had to be stopped. If the police weren't going to stop them, someone had to try.

"True." Mike rested his elbows on his knees. "I'm

betting Vanya could be the key to taking out Polzin. She could break the operation wide open. Do you have any idea what any branch of law enforcement would give to make that arrest?"

"From the look on your face I'd say you'd rank that arrest ahead of Christmas or your birthday."

He sent her a pointed look. "Polzin has a piece of *everything*. On a global scale." The enthusiasm in his voice and the gleam in his eye faded. "That means there's no place for you to hide. It's all or nothing if you intend to be involved in the take down."

For a long moment, she absorbed that news, distancing herself by pretending this was a role, not real life. She was exhausted, mentally and emotionally.

Every discovery left her feeling worse than before. Desmond had died at the hands of a criminal, practically in the arms of an exotic woman with indeterminate loyalties. Feeling hemmed in on all sides, Lauren summoned her courage. "If Vanya's the key, then we need to find her. Maybe she can help us."

"If it was that easy," he argued, "the FBI or Interpol would have done it already."

"I know something they don't."

"Oh yeah, what's that?"

"Vanya is afraid. I saw her fear that night in the office. I might be able to reach her, woman to woman."

MIKE WATCHED Lauren walk out of the office, staring at the empty doorway longer than necessary. There was a lot he could have said in response to her statement. He didn't think it would be easy convincing Vanya to turn on Polzin. Sometimes salvation arrived too late and victims resisted leaving a bad situation.

He shook off the bitterness. This wasn't about his past or those young schoolgirls lost in another country, it was about Lauren's future. To that end, he didn't want Lauren to be part of the search for the woman. Her safety was paramount. Having Vanya's name was a good start. It was only a matter of time before they found a lead on her location. He and Claudia could do this without risk to Lauren. Stopping Polzin was the only way Lauren would ever have any peace. It was also about saving lives.

"Mike? Are you there?" Claudia's voice came through the speakers.

"Yes." He hadn't heard the chime that she'd come online. He swiveled back around and smiled, though the webcams weren't in use. The Guardian Agency prided itself on maintaining anonymity for everyone.

"You could've warned me you'd run me ragged day and night with this one."

"Did you have other plans?" he teased.

"About as often as you do. Missing the surf?"

"Yes."

"Well, if you're not careful, you'll be fish food."

"That's the Italian mob. We're dealing with Russians."

"*Prosti menya*," she said, asking for forgiveness in Russian. "You'll be kneecapped and *then* tossed into the ocean."

He laughed. Hard not to appreciate a woman who knew her criminal disposal protocols. "I'd prefer to take to the ocean on my own terms, knees intact. Based on what you've found, is Vanya enemy or ally?"

"I can't confirm her status just yet." Claudia was silent a long time, but Mike heard the occasional muttering and rattle of her fingers on the keyboard. "Her full name is Vanya Babichev. She's thirty-two."

"How many of us do you support?" he asked, as he scrolled through the Trinity agency blog in search of more clues.

"You're not cleared for that info, Protector Stone."

"Aww. You know I love it when you use my official title."

"Has Lauren identified any other women? Beyond the mistress?"

"A few. All of them are still listed as missing."

"Any of them recent?"

Mike searched his notes. "She remembers seeing one girl in the parking lot at the Trinity Agency building two months ago." He gave her the name. "Did Trinity get a nice chunk of money around that time?"

"Not that I've found," Claudia said, the exasperation coming through loud and clear. "His finances are clean. Nothing in his psych background indicates he'd do this for the fun of it. He was paid, or he was under some sort of pressure."

"We'll find the sweet spot."

"I fear you'll need Vanya for that."

Mike hesitated but only for a second. "I'll make it happen."

"Just don't get dead in the process," Claudia said.

"Would you miss me?"

Claudia snorted and ended the call.

Now all he had to do was figure out how to do this while Lauren stayed here.

Handcuffs could work. *For a number of things.* He chuckled and shook his head. "Get your mind off sex, Stone."

She was a client, temptation be damned, and he was a professional.

East Hollywood, 11:30 p.m.

What the hell had he been thinking?

Lauren had talked him into hitting the clubs in search of Vanya. He had apparently lost his mind. Not true… exactly. Lauren was surprisingly persuasive. And he was increasingly worried about her, the

Russians, and any number of things that could go wrong.

Not that anyone would recognize the sexy actress tonight. The short dark wig and racy clothing was totally un-Lauren-like. She hadn't fallen out of character even once since they left the safe house. Good thing too, because he felt his control slipping with every hour they were together. They'd been working the club scene in this unglamorous part of Hollywood, winding their way deeper into seedy areas.

He couldn't put all the blame for his fraying willpower on the fear of Lauren being discovered. Jealousy reared its ugly head with every appreciative look aimed her way. Maybe he really had lost his mind.

Lauren's full breasts tested the limits of the snug, low-cut dress and yet somehow she kept the effect just shy of trashy. Beside her, he was little more than a prop. They'd been through three clubs and he still hadn't adjusted to being arm candy, to use her term. Whenever men took too much interest, Mike responded with blatantly possessive moves, signaling she was off limits. He had enough to manage as they searched for Vanya. Until getting into a brawl over who would take Lauren home helped their cause, he'd keep himself in check.

He'd certainly had more difficult jobs than spending hours with his eyes and hands all over a gorgeous woman. She played her part perfectly, leaning into his touch, flirting and batting her eyelashes, her breath fanning his ear when she spoke. It was all an act, but his body couldn't seem to remember that detail. Every nuance of her performance drove him closer to the edge, his body craving hers. If they didn't find Vanya soon, he might plead *no mas* and find a private corner just to get a taste of her. He needed some perspective and fast.

"This place has atmosphere, but it's not quite right," she murmured, sipping her overpriced drink while he warned off another potential admirer with a hard look. "But we're getting closer."

Eyeing security cameras in the corners, he considered the scattered details Claudia had on the Krushka syndicate. "One more and we're calling it a night," he reminded her. Disguised or not, staying out too long was dangerous. "We can find another way to get this done."

"Only one more?" She peered up at him through the thick, false eyelashes framing her eyes.

God, she was gorgeous. He kicked the thought out of his head. "We'll go to the Royal and that's it. No negotiations." According to his research, like the last three they'd visited, the Royal had a history of association with Russian mobsters. It was the last one on his list.

"You're the boss," she teased, tapping her fingertip against his lips.

He nipped her finger, pleased when she gasped.

She had to know his self-control was about to snap. He was only human. Holding her gaze, he licked the pad of her finger before letting go. With her body so close to his, the quickening of her breath was obvious. He raised his eyebrows. "Ready to go?"

"Very," she replied, gifting him with another of those secretive, tantalizing smiles.

It was like a punch to the gut. He wanted her to look at him like that and *mean it*. At one time he'd considered himself a good judge of character or at least a good judge of intention. But since he'd come home from his final military assignment, he struggled to trust his instincts when navigating the confusing social games people played. This was one serious game with deadly consequences.

The cool night air cleared his head as they left the club. He tried to hide the dread he felt at starting the charade over at yet another establishment, but they had to play it out. A Hollywood PD car cruised by on patrol and Lauren looked up at him as if he had all of life's answers. Something he couldn't imagine the real, independent Lauren ever doing. At each stop tonight, he'd calculated evasions and exits just in case trouble found them. He didn't relax until the patrol car took the next corner.

When they were settled into a cab and on their way, she squeezed his hand. "I'm having a great time," she said, her eyes sliding to the driver.

"Makes two of us, baby." Holding up his end of the

act, he leaned down and brushed his lips quickly across hers. Big mistake, he thought, as she sucked on her lower lip as if savoring the taste he'd left behind. He was completely outclassed here. Given a choice, he'd tip her back into the seat and feast on that full, sweet mouth until her lips were rosy enough without any gloss or paint.

It was a bitter relief when the cab braked, pulling to a stop at the end of the line where people vied for the doorman's attention.

"Oh, man. Getting into this place doesn't look promising." So far, there hadn't been lines at the other clubs. Odd that this was the hot spot, in this grimy neighborhood.

"Just follow me," Lauren said, already climbing out.

"Hang on." He paid the fare and climbed out after her.

She tossed him a look as the mass of brunette hair swept her cheek. "Trust me."

He didn't have much choice. Feeling like an over-sized accessory, he cooperated as she beamed and sparkled at the ebony-skinned giant guarding the entrance. Those in line watched them closely and he could feel the speculation rippling through the crowd. Mike was working through potential escape routes should any of them guess correctly when the doorman gave a belly laugh and unhooked the velvet rope granting them access.

"What did you say?" Mike asked when they were well inside the retro club.

She trailed a finger along his jaw. "I promised to dump you on the first drunk blonde in here and run away with him."

"God help me."

"Relax, Mike." She patted his cheek. "Part of the fun is being creative."

As soon as he'd recovered from hearing her whisper his name, he muttered, "Fun. Right." They had different definitions. He understood creative as it applied to explosives and combat. Even rescues. He hoped nothing they faced tonight would test those skills.

This club had a vintage 1940's atmosphere with dark wood paneling and sparkling, elaborate chandeliers. There was a wide central floor with plenty of room for people to mingle with a bar along one wall. Heavy velvet drapes framed elevated performance stages. The antique mirrors and sconces added with the deep red and gold accents gave the place a more intimate, gothic feel. Many of the performance stages held gilded cages for the dancers. This had to be the place. As Lauren had said, the others didn't feel right. If the Russian mob kept Vanya working anywhere, Mike would put his money on this club. They squeezed through to order drinks at the bar, then milled and swayed with the crowds mingling between the main dance floor and the bar. He found small relief that most customers were keeping an eye on the DJ or spotlight dancers on the various raised stages. No one seemed overly curious about Lauren.

Vanya wasn't among the spotlighted dancers, but Mike's instincts were on full alert as he noticed a group of men and women in a roped off VIP area. "Recognize anyone?" he asked, slowly shifting to give her a glimpse.

He wasn't sure how he could tell through the makeup and disguise, but the color drained from Lauren's face despite her bright smile. "Kozlov," she said, breathlessly. "Hold me."

Catching the small quiver in her voice and her body, he touched her, silently urging her to keep it together. "I won't let him hurt you," he said at her ear when she leaned her back against him. The move put the ripe curve of her bottom against his groin and he cupped her hips, easing her away before he lost all brainpower.

She swiveled to face him. "I know you won't and I'm grateful."

He didn't want her gratitude. No, he wanted something that wasn't his to claim. This sexy act would be the death of him. "Vanya," he said, with a nod toward an elevated stage as the music changed.

Against his better judgment he turned her, brought her back hard against his chest and rested his hands on her hips while they watched the woman perform. Having Lauren pressed so intimately against him was sweet, tempting torture. If they made it through the night without falling for their own act it would be a miracle.

When the number concluded, Vanya disappeared from the stage.

"There she is," Lauren hissed a moment later, her eyes going wide. "On the last stool. Far end of the bar."

Her excitement was palpable and could blow their cover. "Baby," Mike crooned, brushing his fingertips across the bangs of the brunette wig. "I got it covered."

Her eyes, brown tonight with the contacts, went wide before a seductive smile transformed her face. "Of course you do." Her fingers danced over the buttons of his shirt. "She's alone."

"She only looks that way," he replied.

Lauren gave him a little pout. "Can you give me just a minute with her?" She leaned close, brushing her breasts across his arm, doing a fair job of acting tipsy. "Woman to woman."

He wasn't as optimistic. "Careful what you say," he warned. "I'll be watching."

Her smile turned feline, and then melted away before she meandered through the crowd toward Vanya. Mike followed, taking a different route. He'd give her time, but he wouldn't give the watchdogs room to get between them.

CHAPTER 6

LAUREN TOOK a deep breath and prayed the role she'd sunk into so deeply would hold up for the next few minutes. She couldn't bear to think about the consequences if she failed. Dying would be preferable to being kidnapped by the men who controlled Vanya, who'd murdered Desmond and carried out countless other horrific crimes as a matter of business.

She tapped the bar top and gave Vanya a drunken fan-girl smile. "You're amazing," she gushed. "Did you go to dance school?"

Vanya's lips curved into a bored smile. "For a time I trained in Russia," she said, her accent making every word as exotic as her stunning face. "But all you need to dance here is a feel for the music."

"Oh, don't sell yourself short." Lauren slurred her words a bit. "You have a gift."

Vanya's gaze narrowed and she tossed back whatever had been in her glass. "Excuse me, I must be going."

"Please wait." Lauren stilled her with a light touch on her arm. "I would do *anything* for my boyfriend. He's an agent for a big studio. All… I-I want to do is please him, please help me." She wondered if the stutter would be enough. "I want to learn how to dance your way for him. Do you think of someone special when you dance? Is he here?"

Vanya's dark eyes flared wide and she signaled the bartender for another drink. "And for my friend." She clapped her hand over Lauren's and put her face close enough that they were nearly nose-to-nose. "You must not speak of fairy tales here. They do not end well."

"But it's the city of Angels!" Lauren flung her arms wide and then hugged herself with an exaggerated sigh. "And dreams," she added in a stage whisper. "Let's be best friends. You can show me how to dance and I… I can…" She hiccupped. "I can think of some way to pay you back."

"I know what you're doing," Vanya murmured, her hair like a curtain blocking her profile from the man no doubt watching her every move. "I am no fool, my new friend."

Lauren held her breath. Would she shout for Kozlov now?

Vanya tossed her hair back and raised her glass. "To new friends."

"To new friends," Lauren echoed before downing the shot of vodka. "They help each other," she said, looking down into her glass. She chattered aimlessly until the bartender who'd served them wandered away. "Will you help me? My boyfriend likes your style."

Vanya smiled. "I cannot. You must leave."

Lauren dared to lean closer to her. "But you can help me. I know it." Taking a chance, she let the act fall away. "You could help others, too."

Vanya tossed her hair and laughed, the sound brittle under the pulse of music and loud voices. "You've been out too long tonight, I think. I will give you my remedy for a hangover," Vanya held out her hand. "Give me your phone."

"But the night is young," Lauren complained, dropping the new phone Mike had given her into Vanya's palm.

"If you are lucky there will be other nights, my friend." She returned the phone to Lauren and leaned in to kiss her cheeks in the European tradition. "Andreas would see me dead first. And I am a favorite." Vanya murmured at Lauren's ears. "Do not let my fate become yours." Her gaze drifted behind Lauren and she smiled. "Is this your lady?"

"I hope she isn't pestering you," Mike said. "She really likes your moves."

Vanya beamed at him, but Lauren saw the sadness

in her eyes. "She has my recipe to prevent a hang-over. You will take care of her, yes?"

"Yes. Thank you." Mike put his arm around Lauren and sheltered her as they moved toward the door.

Lauren wanted to protest, to ask for one more minute, but she felt the urgency in his touch, his steps.

He hurried toward the taxi stand and when she shivered, he dropped his suit coat over her shoulders. She pulled it tight letting his scent and the heat from his body envelope her. She'd never felt so safe, despite their walk through a den of vipers. "Thanks."

"We're not clear yet. Laugh."

She laughed on his cue and feigned more of that drunken happiness. They stepped up as the taxi line advanced.

"Lean on me."

She did.

"More. They're watching."

She wasn't sure how much closer she could get, until his arms came around her and he nuzzled her neck. The small touch sent a bolt of delicious heat through her body. They moved forward again. The next cab would carry them away from Vanya, but closer to safety.

Mike opened the door and ushered her in ahead of him. When he settled beside her and the cab pulled away, Lauren saw Kozlov standing by the doorman and pointing their way.

The tremors started in her fingers and her knees felt rubbery. Mike put his arm around her when her teeth began to chatter.

"*Shh.* Should we have a fire when we get home?"

"P-please." If they were going back to the safe house she'd sit right in front of it and not think about how close she'd been to the man who wanted her dead. Or worse—wanted to own her. She told herself he couldn't possibly have recognized her as Lauren Marie Woods. She'd used a different name and identification the entire night. Mike had taken every precaution against being followed. But what if Vanya failed to keep her secret?

"If he knew," Mike said too low for the driver to hear, "it would be obvious by now. Relax."

She couldn't stop herself from twisting around to see if anyone was following them. A few minutes later the cab dropped them in front of a hotel and they walked through the lobby toward the parking garage at the rear. She returned his jacket as they settled into his Camaro.

"You up for a drive?" he asked.

"Please." She was wired and eager to make sense of whatever Vanya had put into the phone.

"You're an excellent drunk," Mike observed, turning west onto Santa Monica Boulevard.

"It helps to be sober." She waited, but he didn't

seem to be in any hurry to call Claudia and she was half afraid to check the message. What if it was only a recipe for a hangover cure? "Are you worried about tonight?"

"No. The disguise held up. You did a great job. I just don't know how productive we've been."

He sounded as weary and frustrated as she felt. "Vanya was receptive. Once she realized who I was." Lauren considered taking off the wig and massaging her scalp, but decided she'd better hold off. "I basically asked her to help me."

"I figured," Mike said. "Kozlov sensed something about the conversation," he added. "They're keeping a close eye on her."

"If she's Polzin's mistress why was she with Desmond that night?"

"Only she knows." Mike drummed his fingertips against the steering wheel.

"One cheek looked bruised to me. She'd done a stellar job with concealer, but I'm certain it was bruised."

"And how are you interpreting that?"

"She's a victim." Lauren raised her chin, daring him to argue. "I think if we can find a way to rescue her, she'd help us."

"No."

Why wouldn't he listen? "That's not the answer I was looking for."

"It's the only answer you're getting tonight."

"Mike, come on. She needs someone."

"I'm here to protect you. From the mob, the police, even from yourself if that's what it takes."

She crossed her arms and leaned as far from him as the car would allow. "Where are we going?"

"There's a quiet spot near the ocean where no one can sneak up on us."

"We aren't overdressed for that at all." But she was already anticipating fresh air and the roar of the surf to chase away the scents of the club clinging to her wig, skin, and clothing.

"I need fresh air," he said, echoing her thoughts. "Go ahead and call Claudia," he suggested. "Get her started on whatever Vanya put into the phone."

"Yes, sir," Lauren muttered, putting the phone on speaker as she entered the contact number she had memorized like a line from a script.

His technical assistant answered immediately. "I've been working the message since it came through," Claudia said. "It's an address embedded in a recipe, I think."

Lauren and Mike exchanged a look, but Lauren recovered first. "You're kidding."

Claudia grumbled incoherently. "Nothing matches up with the little I've gained on her background. Did she say anything helpful?"

Lauren repeated the conversation and Mike chimed in with his observations. Claudia continued to grumble as Mike pulled off the road, parking in a small public lot. He rolled down the windows and they listened to the waves crash into the sand below.

Lauren reviewed the message, while Mike read it over her shoulder. Lauren spotted the problem. "It's not a street address or zip code," she said. "It's written as an acreage address. Search that in Malibu."

"Malibu?" Claudia didn't sound convinced. "Why?"

"Because no one uses Malibu rum as a hangover cure and I remember Desmond talking about researching an area in Malibu as an investment property a few years ago."

As Claudia worked on the other end of the line, they listened to the waves and wind. The sounds were a balm to her overcharged senses. She could happily stay right here all night.

"She's right," Claudia said at last. "I'm sending the actual address to you now and will research the property sale, building codes and such so you can go in prepared."

Mike thanked her and disconnected the call. "There's something else?" he asked, studying Lauren.

She nodded. "I don't think this last line is for cover." Lauren tapped the screen.

"Serves five?" he said, repeating the words on the screen.

She nodded. "I think Vanya is telling us there are five women at this address—possibly the finishing school Desmond talked about—right now." Tears burned in her eyes and she blinked them away, her gaze drifting out over the darkness of the ocean. "I can't believe I was such a fool."

Mike reached out and she let him take her hand, sheltering in in the warmth of his. "We'll figure this out. I promise."

She clamped her lips together and clung to his promise. It was her only lifeline.

MIKE WAS STUNNED that Vanya had possibly given them an address to the school Trinity had mentioned to Lauren. Apparently, the sick bastard had gone through with his plan to create a place to get prospective clients ready for a career in Hollywood. Mike could just imagine what really happened to those women. Beside him, Lauren practically vibrated with what appeared to be an odd mix of despair and excitement. She wanted to end this as badly as he did and he didn't think it was all about reclaiming her career and lifestyle.

As much as he wanted to go in there right now, it was past time to call it a night and return to the hotel Claudia had booked for them as part of tonight's cover. They both needed rest. "We'll come back tomorrow."

"We're close." Lauren's eyes were clear and calm when she met his gaze. "We should do this now."

"It's the middle of the night."

"Isn't that the best time to launch a surprise attack?"

"First we have to recon. We'll get a much better look in the daylight." He could point out that it wouldn't be as simple as knocking on the door, pretending they had car trouble. Deep down she had to know that. Unless his instincts were way off, she was spoiling for a fight and he couldn't blame her.

Anything to burn off the tension. Well, almost anything. The solution a certain part of his anatomy was begging for—getting Lauren naked for a full evaluation of that amazing starlet body—wasn't a valid option.

"We'll take some gear and pretend we're recreational naturalists or something—in the morning."

"If that's your final decision." She exhaled a frustrated breath.

"That's the right decision," he said, his voice gruff. The woman kept him in a constant state of arousal and staying in a room with more bed than floor space wasn't a good idea.

Unfortunately, it was the only option. He didn't see a tail as they drove away from the beach, but that didn't mean it wasn't back there. With Lauren still missing as far as the world knew, Kozlov would keep the entire syndicate on high alert and anyone who'd spoken with Vanya would be thoroughly vetted.

LAUREN DIDN'T APPRECIATE BEING CUT off, even if he was right. It felt like he was shooting down every suggestion she made. He might be the expert, but she had skills, too. Skills she'd put to excellent use tonight. A streetlight's reflection glared across the sparkling beads on her skirt and she sighed. There was no denying they were dressed for clubbing, not scoping out what could be a trap. She didn't want to believe Vanya would do that, but then again, Polzin's mistress wasn't in total control of the situation. After all, she had told the police a pack of lies about what happened in Desmond's office.

By the time they reached their hotel room, Lauren had reconciled to the idea of waiting until tomorrow to make a move. "As long as we're resting up for tomorrow, food would be good, too."

"Name your take out."

"Chinese." At least she'd get a wealth of cooked veggies that way. Thinking of food made her wonder about the conditions at the school. "How often do you think they bring food in to the women they keep at the school?"

"Alleged school," he reminded her.

She huffed in exasperation. "Allegedly, how often do you think they take food in?"

"Are you thinking we might be able to sneak the victims out on a food truck?"

"We might have better luck with a laundry cart. It's a classic tactic for a reason." She could tell by his quick flash of a smirk he found her Hollywood suggestion amusing. Her attempt at humor didn't last long as worry crept in again. "It must be something like a prison."

"Whatever the setup, it's probably self-sufficient," he replied.

Lauren hid her dismay behind a tacit agreement. They'd find out tomorrow. Though daylight was only a few hours away, it felt like far too long to wait. "Can we tell the police about the school?" she asked when they were back in the hotel suite. "Couldn't they investigate?"

He picked up the stack of laminated menus near the room phone and handed them to her. "What place and with what cause? We don't know anything yet. And let's not forget that we don't know who we can trust inside the police department."

"Maybe Claudia's property research will give us options."

"That's possible. We'll check it out tomorrow and go from there."

Lauren had to forcibly ignore the way his shoulders flexed as Mike removed his jacket. His fingers worked the buttons at his cuffs and he rolled the fabric back over his forearms. When had that become so sexy?

Maybe when she was desperate to do anything but think about waiting for tomorrow.

The meager splash of charm he rationed with that ripped body and sexy swagger made him nearly irresistible. She couldn't remember the last time she'd been so attracted to a man. Blaming the lure of him on stress and proximity wasn't working anymore. In the clubs tonight she could've had her choice of tempting men, but she'd only wanted Mike and not just for safety or protection. Maybe it was the reality that she hadn't had sex in two years.

Two whole years. The passing brush of a kiss and touch of a hand in public was all she and Desmond had shared on a physical level since she'd discovered his penchant for cheating. She was not only in serious trouble here, she was truly pathetic.

"Call in an order for whatever you want to eat," he said. "Use my name and credit card. I'm grabbing the first shower." He closed the door before she could reply.

Staring at the closed door, she cursed the years she'd wasted with Desmond. Their dysfunctional relationship had messed with her head and undermined her confidence. She did the necessary maintenance on and off camera to keep her job and to audition for others, all the while telling herself Desmond would come around. That he cared for her in his odd way. And he did, twisted as that care was. He'd kept her employed and, as his loyal girlfriend, he kept her visible among the media. He'd told her the other women were meaningless. Vanya might not have been important to Desmond personally, but she was essential to sorting this out. Lauren knew it with every fiber of her being, even if she didn't have proof. Yet. As soon as the woman had recognized Lauren, something in her eyes had changed.

How bizarre was it that the two things she and Vanya had in common were Desmond and his murder? Only Vanya was the witness and possible other woman, while Lauren was the girlfriend and person of interest. She should be angry that the other woman had put her in this position, but somehow she wasn't. They had both been deceived and used by ruthless men. Who knew if either of them would survive what was to come?

Lauren's gaze drifted to the closed bathroom door. As awful as all this was, if it hadn't happened she wouldn't have met Mike, a man she wanted to know beyond his abilities as an investigator and bodyguard. That startling thought shook her. Now who was twisted? This wasn't the right time for silver linings and happily-ever-afters. They were both in a great deal of danger and if there really were women being held hostage at the address Vanya provided, they both needed help.

"Lauren?"

She jumped at the firm tone and gentle shake of her shoulder that broke into her thoughts. She stared at him, and then did a double take. Mike wore nothing but a towel slung low across his lean hips and her body responded, instantly. She closed her eyes, but it was too late. Some things couldn't be unseen. Not that she'd suffer if this particular image haunted her for a lifetime.

His torso would've kept Leonardo da Vinci enthralled for hours, it was so perfectly defined. Dark hair dusted his pecs and speared down past his navel, disappearing under the towel. She jerked her gaze back up, studying the tattoo of an elaborate compass star that decorated the left side of his chest.

"You're... fit," she blurted awkwardly. "Excuse me." She stumbled toward the desk chair. "I'll just make that call for the food now."

"I would've dressed, but you didn't answer. When I turned off the water it was too quiet in here. I called your name several times."

She used the menu as a fan, vainly trying to cool the embarrassment heating her cheeks. There was no point denying her obvious attraction to him. "I was just thinking. I'm okay."

"All right." He returned to the bathroom and fool that she was, she watched him go. He moved with such stealth and grace. "I was worried you'd left," he said with a glance over his shoulder.

She shook her head. "You're stuck with me." And now she was stuck with the delectable image of his flawless body seared into her memory. When she felt like she could place the order in a normal voice, she called it in.

The task done, she searched for another distraction. Anything to keep from staring at the perfectly good bed in the room. She'd done love scenes, on the soap and in movies. Giving viewers the gasps, grasps, and glimpses they wanted meant leaving modesty in the dust. Despite sheets and modesty panels, exposure was part of the process on a set.

When hunky men were slated for love scenes, it seemed like every woman involved with a studio created a reason to slip into the closed set. It made her unreasonably jealous thinking of Mike in the role of leading man, being ogled by strangers. How odd— especially considering he wasn't an actor and they weren't a couple.

What was wrong with her brain tonight? "I'm being ridiculous," she muttered, pushing to her feet. On instinct she moved to the window and caught herself just before she opened the curtains. They couldn't take a chance that someone had followed them and might be watching.

"Restless?" Mike asked, his deep voice drifting across her senses.

"You have no idea," she replied, refusing to turn around.

"You might be surprised," he said. "Come sit down, Lauren."

She closed her eyes. There wasn't much choice. It

was either stare at the curtains, counting the swoops and flowers in the fabric, or be a grown up and deal with the situation. She was an accomplished actress, surely she could pull off being indifferent rather than insanely attracted to the man hired to protect her.

With a polite smile, she turned and her mouth went dry as she enjoyed the view. He lounged in the upholstered chair on the far side of the room, his legs stretched out and crossed at the ankle. Dressed in faded jeans and a black t-shirt, his feet still bare, and his damp hair pushed back from his face, he mesmerized her.

"I won't deny there's something electric between us," he said. "Under different circumstances, I might make a move." His brow lined in concern. "You should sit down."

On automatic pilot, she obeyed the softly spoken order, sinking into the desk chair, clasping her hands in her lap. Where had she left the menu fan when she needed it all over again?

"What you're feeling is common."

She bristled, exasperated with what felt like yet another loop through the cycle that originated back in Kansas with her father-knows-everything upbringing. "What do you think I'm feeling?"

"You said you did research for your role as Dr. Loveless."

She nodded, more curious than she should be about where he was headed with this conversation.

"Did you get to the psych chapter on sex being a primal response to adrenaline, death, and loss?"

"Are you suggesting we sleep together so I'll feel better?" She was remarkably okay with the idea.

"No." He leaned forward, bracing his elbows on his widespread knees, a wicked gleam in his deep blue eyes. "I'm suggesting the urge to jump me is natural."

"That's some academy-award winning arrogance, Mike."

He arched an eyebrow. "You shouldn't dwell on it or stress about it," he continued. "I'm convenient and—"

She tipped her head back and laughed. "You're nothing close to convenient. I can't argue the attraction is there. Good Lord, you're better than gorgeous and built like Adonis. You've got the preserve and protect routine down to a science. I'm sure it would be a memorable experience." She aimed a glance toward the bed. "But you're right, I can't dwell on that. More importantly, I won't use you as a distraction from my problems."

He leaned back, studying her with a deep frown. "I'm glad we're on the same page."

"Did I hurt your feelings?" She'd called him Adonis for heaven's sake. That kind of compliment should soothe any man's ego. He had a mirror, and she was well aware how much effort went into maintaining that kind of physique.

He rolled his eyes. "Of course not."

"But there's something else you wanted to say."

"No." His gaze skated over her body. "How long until the food gets here?"

She prayed one day a man would look at her with that quiet intensity and stick around long enough to convince her to take the leap. And it would take convincing because she just didn't trust her ability to make smart decisions when it came to men anymore. Desmond, may he rest in peace, had ruined that for her. Checking the clock near the bed, she shrugged. "Soon I hope."

Her stomach growled and they both smiled a little. A quick change of subject was in order. She wanted to talk about Vanya, but their visit to the club was too charged with that chemistry and attraction he spoke so clinically about. She'd never go clubbing again, not even out for drinks, without thinking of her body softening against his rock-hard form. "Have you ever thought of stunt work?"

"No." He sat up a little. "That's not exactly true. When I first came home a friend, Hank Patterson, got me a gig consulting on an action movie with a military plot."

"He's married to Sadie McClain."

"HE IS," Mike confirmed. "The pay was good and the hours weren't bad, but it just wasn't my thing."

That raised a tide of questions, but she clamped her mouth shut. At the knock on the room door, she followed his silent signal, waiting in the bathroom while he paid for the food. For several wonderful minutes she dug into fried rice, noodles, and spicy chicken and didn't think of murder or mobsters at all.

When he loaded his paper plate with a second helping, she asked, "Tell me about coming home again to California. The consulting."

"You'll be offended."

"Lame excuse." She wouldn't let him evade. "Keep going."

"After leaving my SEAL team abruptly, I wasn't good at trusting people. The schedule on the set was fine, the work itself was fine, but the social aspect was too much."

She knew what he wasn't saying. "The actresses fell all over you."

"Maybe."

She circled her plastic fork in the air. "The face and eyes are more than enough. Add in the body and being the new guy in town and that's an irresistible combination in Hollywood."

"Voice of experience?"

She bobbed her chin. "There are days this place feels like little more than a civilized freak show for beautiful people. You do know that guys have work done to look like you."

"Is that another compliment?"

She grinned. "Definitely." It should be the last one. For all she knew giving him three compliments in a row would erode the remnants of her self-control. Silly yes, but she wasn't ruling it out. "Go on."

"I wasn't a fool," he declared, setting his plate down and taking a long drink from his bottled water. "This kind of talk should come with a beer."

"Then you should've shared last night," she said. "Quit stalling and just tell me who you slept with."

"None of them." His voice flat, he scowled at a point on the wall behind her. "I couldn't tell who was real and who was fake."

It wouldn't have been a concern for most men. Men or women, actually. Most people wouldn't care about real or fake if it meant spending private time with a man like Mike. The admission only confirmed her opinion about his integrity and good character, though it seemed to drag him into a pit full of bad memories. She wanted to soothe, to tell him whatever had happened didn't matter. She wanted to make them both forget for just a little while, but she didn't want her gesture to be misunderstood.

"In the Navy, I trusted other men with my life," he said. "Men who'd step in front of a bullet to save a friend or the operation without a second thought. Men who never left a brother behind." He picked up a wrapped fortune cookie and just turned it around and around in his hands. "Knowing real from fake was part of the job. We learned when people were lying, knew how to distinguish the truth with or without supporting intel."

She held her breath, afraid any sound or movement would interrupt him.

"My team had bad intel on my last operation. I can't go into all the details, but we handled it. Rescued fifteen young girls and their teacher from a terrorist attack. But someone had to be the scapegoat when things went crazy and all too political."

"You volunteered." It was so clear to her, the resignation and grief stamped on his face. He'd stepped in front of a problem as lethal as a bullet to cover a friend.

He nodded absently. "None of us did anything wrong but by the time we got there, a few victims had been, well, turned is the best word. We encountered unexpected resistance. Like I said, we handled it," he repeated, his gaze haunted. "As a team. But after the fact, our actions got the wrong attention. When the team comes back without a scratch, but the hostages appear to have been caught in friendly fire, someone has to take the blame. I was single with no one else counting on my paycheck or benefits so I stepped up. Deep down I didn't really expect to be booted from the SEAL program." When he lifted his head and met her gaze his eyes were clear again.

"When my tour was up, I came home and started over, but I didn't like not knowing who to trust. It bothered me that I'd lost that ability."

"You didn't lose that skill," she stated firmly. "You were a successful bounty hunter in the Angeles Forest case."

"I caught the killer, but I damn well misjudged the sheriff and his need to pretend it was a one-man operation—his. Even that wasn't enough for him. He tried his level best to make anything that had gone wrong look as if it was my fault." He picked up his plate and carried it to the trashcan.

She didn't know what to say, didn't have the expertise to offer him comfort he wouldn't brush off. "And the Guardian Agency?"

"They found me right after the Angeles Forest press conference."

The same press conference she recalled so vividly. "You trust them." It made her sad that he'd done good things, noble things, and still carried around these burdens from his past.

"It's good work. The money always comes through. Claudia always answers the call if I need assistance." He hooked his thumbs in his back pockets. "Besides, I didn't have anything more to lose. I was too far gone down the wrong path."

"That's a scary place." She thought she'd hit that kind of low after her mom died. Until she became a person of interest in a murder case, sought by the police and the real killers. The nonsense she'd gone through with her father might have been equally hurtful, but it hadn't posed the same risk to her entire existence. Sitting here at a new all-time low, she abruptly understood there was far more to lose.

Her steady work, sure, but that felt trivial in comparison to what the women who might be trapped in Polzin's operation would lose. She hated Desmond for being part of it.

And Mike… she needed his help without a doubt. If her situation spilled over and hurt him, she'd never shake that burden. A good friend or psychologist would probably tell her she was taking on too much that wasn't her responsibility. Too bad. She wouldn't stop until those women were safe.

"I bummed you out," Mike said, watching her closely.

"No." She managed to force her lips into a smile. "How could your story do anything but inspire me?" Rising from the chair, she crossed the room. Keeping her eyes on his, she reached up and laid her hands on his cheeks, the stubble of his whiskers rasping against her palms. He didn't resist when she drew his face close, but he didn't touch her.

She pressed her lips to his and the first contact was soft, sweet, and warm. Her eyes still open, she watched something spark in those midnight-blue depths. Her body responded, fanning that spark to a hot blaze and she felt a soul-deep recognition of someone who would either complete her or shatter her. She stepped back, uncertain of the next step.

"That's some academy-award winning tender-ness," he whispered, paraphrasing her earlier words. "No need to keep up the act now."

She almost snapped, angry that he'd try to ruin the moment, before she realized the classic defensive maneuver. Instead of words, she'd give him the truth in a more visceral way. She kissed him again, this time giving him a small taste of the desire pounding through her blood. If she had a magic wand, she'd erase his lingering doubt and frustration. He hadn't failed anyone, no matter what the official documents or the media said to the contrary.

His hands landed on her waist and she lost the ability to think clearly. His fingers curling into the fabric of her dress, he changed the angle of the kiss. She sighed and his tongue, laced with hot spices from his meal, swept into her mouth, tipping her world upside down.

She clutched his shoulders for balance. He was her anchor in a sudden storm of longing that slammed her from every side. It was too much of the unexpected, more intense as one sensation after another crackled through her.

With her last shred of self-preservation, she eased back and the strong arms that had banded around her fell away.

They stared at each other for a long moment. She

wouldn't call it a mistake, though it must have been. She should apologize, but she wasn't the least bit sorry and wouldn't spoil the moment with a lie. He'd just told her he wanted someone real.

Which left... what? Her mind couldn't come up with another option, her thoughts caught in a whirlwind of happy, girlish endorphins. Finally, she forced herself to move, to break the invisible tether holding her in place, and retreated to the privacy of the bathroom. She might just stay in here until morning, except that felt cowardly.

Behind the safety of the closed door, she pressed her fingers to her tingling lips. If something happened to Mike in the process of saving her she would know an entirely new lifelong torture.

She splashed cool water on her face and then gave in and took a cold shower. He'd probably decided she was a tease. Whether it was chemistry, adrenaline, or outright attraction, she couldn't risk acting on it now. It would be more than unfair—to both of them. It would be irresponsible to create a potential distraction. She might not have his experience with criminals or investigations, but it was common sense if two people relying on each other suffered a breach of communication, things would go from bad to worse in a hurry.

She'd been a fool once already.

On the set, the director simply ordered another take. But in their very real situation the slightest problem could mean failure for the missing women, Mike, or an innocent bystander. She didn't want that kind of disaster on her conscience.

And she didn't want to ever give him a reason to call whatever this was between them a mistake.

CHAPTER 7

Malibu, Friday, December 12, 5:20 a.m.

Mike was up before the sun and longing for an hour with his surfboard. He needed the constancy of the ocean, the surge of the tide. There'd been no nightmare despite talking about his last mission and the subsequent fallout. He needed space to think about what that meant, although after that mind-blowing kiss he wasn't sure thinking was possible.

He'd given her a wide berth when she'd come out of the bathroom and he'd refused to hear any argument when he'd told her to take the bed while he slept on the floor. Amazingly, he'd even succeeded in keeping his eyes on his laptop when he heard her sliding under the covers. His prayers that she'd fall asleep quickly weren't answered, but that was no surprise. At least she hadn't wanted to talk about the kiss or anything else.

Turning to the bed, he watched her sleep and marveled at the view. She was lovely and so much deeper than he'd expected of a woman in her line of work. He rubbed his eyes. When a man stared at a sleeping woman without thinking about sex, he was in big trouble. Now he sounded like his old man— never a good thing. What a jacked up mess he was making of the situation. His job here—his only job— was to keep her safe until the bad guys were in custody. End of story. The problem with that neat ending was the glaring fact that the bad guys would never be in custody unless the two of them made it happen. Making it happen was where things got tricky.

Reclaiming a small bit of focus, he set up the coffee machine for her. Sliding into his shoes he grabbed his wallet and a room key before heading to the vending machine for his morning cola. He'd accused her of acting just to keep her at arm's length. What a dumb move that had been. She'd taken it well, but she deserved his apology for that petty attack. He would do that, he vowed, just as soon as she brought up the subject of the kiss. He popped the top on the can of cola and drained half of it. Why was he afraid of a simple conversation? Of a heartfelt kiss?

The answer would take far more time than he had at the moment.

She was awake when he came back in and cradling her cup of coffee between her hands. "Thanks for this," she said, raising the cup. "Did you sleep okay?"

The gratitude shining in her pale eyes made him feel as if he'd slayed a dragon. "I did." He drained the rest of his cola, eager for the infusion of sugar and caffeine. He held up his phone. "Email from Claudia. She went back over the travel routines of a few groups who deal…" He hesitated.

"In women," Lauren filled the gap.

He nodded. "Seems several of them are in the area. She did some backtracking and California is an annual stop this time of year."

"I can't believe I didn't pick up on this." She closed her eyes for a second. "I keep telling myself I'm not going to dwell on my ignorance and yet here I am beating that dead horse again," she griped, striding across the room to her bag. "If we're reading Vanya's coded message correctly, there are five women waiting at Desmond's so-called finishing school for pick-up. Maybe the school is one of the annual stops."

He agreed, but they needed to approach their next step with extreme caution. "Let's go be naturalists then. No wig, but wear your hair up with a hat or something."

"Yes, sir." She tossed him a mock salute, grabbed her clothes and headed for the bathroom.

He used the time to prepare and order room service for breakfast. An hour later they were geared up and following the navigation prompts toward the address in a canyon outside Malibu.

In the car with the windows rolled down to enjoy the crisp winter morning, Mike relaxed. It helped just getting away from the temptation of Lauren in the hotel suite with that huge bed. The ocean breeze was a welcome distraction from her enticing scent. He had to get her out of his head. She was a client. He didn't allow clients to get under his skin.

"We'll drive by and then double back," he said as the computerized voice announced the next turn on their route. "I don't want to make anyone suspicious."

"Do you think it's like a prison?"

He'd been considering that. "Out here it could be nothing more than a glorified shipping container."

"How awful." The agony in her voice made it clear she was still blaming herself for not seeing through Trinity.

"The most successful organized crime rings are ruthless. It's why they succeed. They fool a lot of people, Lauren. They're very good at making sure no one sees the ugliness except the victims." For all he knew Trinity was a victim as well, being manipulated against his better judgment. Mike couldn't bring himself to defend the man.

"I get the theory," she muttered. "I don't have to like it."

She watched the map on his navigation system while he watched the real road. "It's remarkably isolated out here," he said. He shouldn't have been surprised, but when it seemed as if every square inch of available land was under development, areas like this one were an unusual sight.

"That's it," he said. They passed the turn off and the computerized version of Claudia's voice filled the car with suggestions, rerouting them back to the destination.

Lauren twisted in her seat, straining for a glimpse. "Nothing but road."

He didn't see any type of security or guard at the intersection, but he supposed the Dead End and No Trespassing signs hanging off the gate deterred the majority of recreational drivers. "We'll have a better view from the rise in a few minutes." He pressed a button on the steering wheel and called Claudia. When she answered, he asked, "Anything more on the ownership of the school?"

"Good morning to you, too."

"Sorry," he said. "I could lose the signal any time."

"I've been at it all night." Claudia ignored his excuse. "At first glance, the land is owned by the county and protected for wildlife."

"Where were those officials when the Russian mob started using the property?"

"Looking the other way with a fistful of cash, I..."

Claudia's voice faded away as the signal was lost.

"Damn." Mike glanced at Lauren. "Don't worry, she'll have answers when we get back to the hotel."

Lauren drummed her fingertips on her knees. "Maybe we'll bust them for zoning violations."

Mike laughed. "You've got a point. They got Al Capone on tax evasion."

The levity didn't last. When the silence had gone on too long, he chased it away with a promise. "I won't let you take the rap for Trinity's murder."

"You're sure we shouldn't go to the police? Officer Cooper would listen."

"He might listen," Mike said as he pulled the car to the side of the road. "The news alert on my phone still shows you're a wanted person of interest. Officer Cooper can't protect you from Kozlov and the syndicate needs your silence. If Cooper thought the LAPD was your best bet, he wouldn't have recommended the Guardian Agency in the first place." Mike cut the engine and gave her a reassuring smile. "Grab a camera and let's go see what kind of view we have of this finishing school."

When she stepped out of the car she looked like the perfect tourist with her ponytail threaded through the back of her ball cap and the camera around her neck. A bag designed to carry extra lenses was slung across her body, emphasizing the fullness of her breasts. Mike gave himself a mental slap as he hooked his small pack over one shoulder. Stocked with binoculars, surveillance devices, his handgun, ammo, and a couple bottles of water, he was as set as he could be. She impressed him, matching his pace while they hiked up the rise and then dropping into a crouch, keeping low until they could see the building below.

"That's it?" Astonishment filled her tone. "It looks real. Like a small private school campus."

"It is real," he said.

She bumped her shoulder against his. "You know what I mean. It looks respectable. Permanent."

He kept his opinion to himself until she realized what she'd said.

"This isn't a setup that came into existence just a few months ago. They've been doing this… for years." She groaned. "I'm going to be sick."

"That won't help us or anyone inside."

With the binoculars, he studied the setup. One road in. A small gravel parking lot wrapped around the tidy, two story building. From this angle they could see the rear, west end, and front of the building. No windows on the first floor at the back or side of the building, but plenty on the second floor. Windows flanked the double front door. The only other visible door was on the west end facing their position. Mike's money had been on modified shipping containers or even the temporary offices used at construction sites. But Lauren nailed it with 'permanent'. The building was even up to code with a fire escape that led to a second story door on the west end.

Mike lowered his binoculars. "I'm going in. If you hear any trouble, drive back down to where you have cell service and call Claudia. She'll know what to do. Another protector—"

"I'm going with you."

He clenched his jaw, biting back his impatience. "You don't have the skills for this and I won't subject you to more danger." Regardless of last night's success, they had gotten far too close to Kozlov.

"You have the skills to cover both of us." Her conviction was almost contagious. "I'm going in. With you or after you're inside, your choice."

"Hold on a minute and let's think this through." He paused, taking his own advice to prevent a pointless argument. "The truck and the sedan parked near the side entrance indicate at least two people inside. Guards or staff of some sort. Let's watch for a bit to see if we can spot any movement."

"I can do that." She snapped a few pics with the camera.

As he studied the landscape and the building more closely, he appreciated her affinity for silence. The side door opened and a man stepped outside. He walked over to the truck, leaned against the tailgate, and lit a cigarette. His white polo shirt and dark jeans looked normal enough, but the heavy-soled work boots and semi-automatic weapon at his hip weren't standard for most finishing school teachers.

From behind her camera Lauren gasped.

"You recognize him?" Would they be that lucky?

"No," she whispered. "Do you see that gun?"

"Yes," Mike replied. "The only reason the guard would be armed is if there's something inside that needs to be protected... or kept under control." It looked as if Vanya had come through.

"What now?"

"Let him finish his cigarette." He needed the time to think. "Then we'll find a way in."

"What about cameras, motion sensors, or other guards?"

He lowered the binoculars and caught her gaze. "Good question. No cameras or sensors that I can see. Whatever they're up to, they're damned confident nothing can touch them out here. I'm hoping we can get in through the fire escape door."

"Let's do it."

Her words made him smile in spite of himself. He wouldn't insult her bravery or downplay her dedication again, though he didn't want her being too brave or dedicated and getting herself hurt or killed.

"When we go in," he'd resigned himself to her joining him, "you have to do exactly what I tell you. Otherwise you could get yourself or one of the women inside killed."

"I won't ask questions or argue with you. Promise."

He hoped for the sake of everyone involved, she'd keep that promise. "Whatever we find, we're only gathering information." He might plant some listening devices, but she didn't need to worry about that part.

"What if we find the women in there?"

He shook his head. "This isn't a rescue. Yet," he added when she started to protest. "Reconnaissance first, then action with the right kind of backup. We don't want to be the reason anyone dies today."

She shuddered. "Got it."

As they made their way down the hillside, Mike mentally prepared for the worst. The absence of cameras and any other sort of sensors on the exterior of the building gave him pause. Anything that looked this easy rarely was.

When they reached the west end of the building Mike jumped up and caught the pull-down ladder of the fire escape. The creak as it slid to the ground made him wince. Since the guard didn't burst through the door right next to him, he was able to breathe again. He hustled up the ladder first with Lauren right behind him. On the landing he fished his lock pick set from the pack. It took a good thirty seconds but the tumblers finally released. Now if only there was no security sensor on the door.

They'd soon know. Mike grasped the knob, gave it a twist, and eased the door inward…

No screaming siren and no thudding sound of boots rushing closer. Relieved, he surveyed the room. Big, square, and empty. One wall was mirrored and ballet bars were mounted on the wall opposite.

"Dance studio," she whispered, a furrow appearing between her pale eyebrows.

He nodded. Crossing to the doorway, he paused to listen. Met with silence, he eased the door open and stepped into a long corridor. Doors lined both sides. He pressed a finger to his lips and moved forward. Lauren followed.

It was a serious risk, but he peered through the window of the first door. A young woman paced the small room the size of a prison cell. The window in the door was one-way glass he realized when she paused, stared at the door but didn't react to seeing his face there. The room was sparse, furnished with only a narrow cot and a change of clothes hanging on the wall. There in the far right corner near the ceiling was a camera, its red light indicating it was live. He'd figured there had to be some electronic security around here. On the wall to the right of the door was an intercom box with a call button. A way for the prisoner to let the guard know she needed something, he supposed. He moved aside so Lauren could see. She pressed a hand over her mouth to hold in her reaction.

Again he pressed a finger to his lips to remind her that absolute quiet was essential. She nodded and they moved past five more rooms, three of them occupied by pretty young women. Since all but one of the rooms had a change of clothes hanging on the wall, Mike decided there were likely a total of five prisoners—which seemed to confirm the information Vanya had passed along. There was a common bathroom and what might have been a central lounge if it had been furnished. Midway along the corridor a stairwell led downward, presumably to the first level. At the far end of the corridor was a well-equipped gym just as deserted as the dance studio they'd entered.

Frantic piano notes drifted from somewhere downstairs. Mike exchanged a look with Lauren, but her face reflected his confusion. He headed for the stairwell and started down, pausing on each step to listen. The player struggled to bring a classical composition out of a piano with a halting, jerky touch. Maybe prisoner number five was having a piano lesson.

As promised, Lauren followed him without a word. They stopped on the stairs when the piano went silent, moving again when the music swelled, played by a master this time. Mike gave Lauren a signal to wait as they reached the first floor landing, and then he inched around the corner and had a look.

More doors lined the corridor but all were closed and none had windows. He eased back out of sight when he heard boots squeaking across the waxed floors. Lauren watched him with wide eyes, but she didn't speak.

A phone rang nearby, the shrill sound doing the piano student no favors. The booted feet quickened and a man's voice answered the summons in a foreign language. Definitely Russian. Mike couldn't catch anything helpful from the conversation. He hadn't spotted any cameras in the corridors, but he didn't want to take the risk of being discovered and dropping Lauren right into their laps. He planted a bug under the handrail at the bottom of the staircase as well as another under a table near the front door, and then he ushered Lauren silently back up the steps.

They left the building just as they'd entered and moved quickly back up the hill. He programmed a receiver and transmission booster for the bugs, confident Claudia would be able to make sense of any intel. He knew from previous cases that she had state of the art translation software.

The arrogance of the operation disgusted him almost as much as the trafficking. None of the women had exhibited signs of physical torture, but an expert could inflict pain and exert control without leaving visible evidence. The four women he had seen looked to be in their very early twenties. All appeared resigned to their fate. If Trinity had been funneling women to Polzin like this for years…

Good thing someone else had already killed him because Mike would have gladly done so himself.

"We have to get them out," Lauren said when they reached their hiding place at the top of the ridge. "There's what? Three guards on site watching them?"

"At least three and possibly a piano teacher." Not bad odds. "We won't be making a move like that this morning."

"But they could be moved, sold, or whatever at any time."

"I know." His hands in tight fists, he wanted to attack as well. Images and sounds from that rescue in Mumbai kept playing in his brain. These bastards were no better than the sons of bitches who had taken all those young girls from that school on the other side of the world. The situation was too similar for Mike's comfort. Though the political fallout wasn't an issue here, there was plenty of room for error. What if some of these captives didn't want to be free either? He had to allow for that, even as he tried to keep the past from interfering with his decisions in the present. When captives were held long enough, and brainwashed adequately, they didn't always understand what was best for them.

"We need a plan and more information. This goes beyond rescuing those five women. We need to make the connection between these women and Polzin. We need to shut down this operation."

"I'll give you a plan." She flung her arm toward the school. "We go in and subdue the guards. We hold the building until the police arrive."

"And then what? Hope those women are able and willing to identify who took them and why? We have no proof of why they're here much less that they're prisoners. We can't prove this isn't some weird rehab."

"Vanya said—"

"Do you think the police—*good* cops—will get here before a Russian crew?" He cut her off. Hell, he was sorely tempted to do as she asked, but if they failed… "We only know this piece of the puzzle. Even if we're damned lucky, the most we can hope for is that the police will close five missing-person cases, but that doesn't save you or any of the other women who've already been victims of these bastards. It's possible whoever they've turned inside the police department could ensure we're ushering them into a death sentence." He pushed a hand through his hair. They had to be smart here.

For several seconds she simply stood there staring at him, and then she spoke. "Mike?"

"I'm thinking." He yanked himself back to the present. "Even if we get those women to the police, Kozlov and everyone involved in the Polzin operation is still out there. They can lay low, like Trinity suggested before he died, and come back stronger. They'd definitely come back with a bigger axe to grind against you."

"Right now I don't care about me. I care about saving those women."

"All right." He planted his hands at his waist. "What do you want?"

"What do you mean?" She glared at him.

"Do you want to save five women or do you want to end the operation?"

"Both," she snapped.

Had he expected a different answer? "Then we wait and we watch."

"And plan," she said. She wheeled around, dropped her camera bag and stretched out on the ground. She dragged out her binoculars and focused on the school.

Without a better option at the moment, he joined her. Maybe they'd get lucky and observe some definitive action soon. At least the perception of doing something was good for Lauren's morale. At some point he'd have to make the decision to go in with or without a connection to the men in charge.

An epiphany had him shaking his head. Here he'd thought he was in charge when the fact of the matter was that his decisions lately were based on keeping her happy as well as safe. He was a professional— usually. He didn't know why this woman had such an effect on him. Beautiful didn't begin to describe the light and energy inside her. She was so much more than her perfect features and tantalizing body.

He liked her mind, even when she challenged the orders he gave for her safety. He liked her mind? What the hell? With a mental groan, he focused on the school and the case. She wanted to save these young women and to take down an established crew of human traffickers. He supported the concept, but that kind of operation usually required extensive preparation and observation before law enforcement stormed in with cuffs and arrest warrants. Lauren was a client caught in no-win land between the police and a deadly mob. She had a good heart, valiant intentions, and he was here to protect her from danger. If only he could protect her from him.

He removed headphones and a small dish from his pack, setting it up so they could catch any conversations that might take place outside. "We might not get as much as we'd like to today."

"We already know more than we did when we woke up this morning," she murmured. "And there's plenty of day left."

He didn't challenge her. They didn't have another lead and it wasn't safe to go back to the club. The memory of that snug dress had him fighting off another ill-timed erection. To do this right they needed Kozlov or his boss to show up here. Who knew when or if that would happen?

"Righting a wrong is a good thing," he said,

tapping his boot to her tennis shoe. Even that small contact had his mind drifting down inappropriate paths. "Taking on Trinity's guilt isn't."

"That's not it," she protested.

He waited.

"Maybe that's part of it." She went quiet for a moment. "There's so much crap in the world," she said. "What's wrong with wanting to clean up this particular corner?"

"Nothing." He'd shared the perspective way back before he learned the hard way that truth and justice didn't always win. Bad people and the crap they dumped on the world had a way of sprouting back up. "As long as you live long enough to appreciate the effort."

"I'm aware Polzin isn't the only criminal involved with human trafficking, that a global problem won't end with him. But letting him continue to profit when we have at least some tangible evidence that might stop him isn't acceptable to me."

"Fair enough." It helped to know that, besides a soft heart, she had a bigger goal than simply appeasing misplaced guilt. And it did ridiculous things to his ego that she thought he had the skill and smarts to take down even a piece of the Krushka syndicate.

"I hear a vehicle," she whispered.

"Got 'em." Mike aimed his binoculars at a long black limousine, the two escorting SUVs, and another smaller sedan. The vehicles rounded the last curve of the canyon road and proceeded into the parking lot below. Kozlov got out of one of the SUVs and stalked toward the limo. Anticipation whipped through Mike as he heard Lauren's camera working. The limo driver emerged and moved swiftly to open the back door for his passenger.

A tall man exited the limo and Mike zeroed in on his face. "Holy hell. That's Andreas Polzin." Federal law enforcement would do backflips if they knew the bastard was in the States. The local situation must be seriously jacked up if the syndicate boss was personally tending this twig on his sprawling criminal tree. It was one thing to visit the mistress, another to inspect what amounted to a holding yard. Men like Polzin usually steered clear of the day-to-day activities.

If Lauren had stayed at the hotel, Mike might've waded in and removed a few players in this drama, but he didn't want her anywhere near these men. Taking a swipe at Polzin's personnel might be satisfying, but it wouldn't make enough of a difference. There were too many men eager to move up the food chain and step into a vacated position.

Polzin walked through the front door held open by one of the men standing guard and Mike took a deep breath. With any luck they'd have a conversation in English near one of the bugs he'd planted.

"Why would Vanya let herself be used by him?" Lauren asked. "He's pure evil."

"The real question is whether she'll let *us* use her," Mike replied.

"She gave us the school," Lauren said. "Besides, we want to help her, not use her."

He marveled at Lauren's bright and shiny idealism. That sort of thinking had been drummed out of him by the time he finished his first SEAL mission. Helping them bring Trinity's killer to justice would effectively end Vanya's way of life. He knew firsthand how much people resisted change, especially if you couldn't show them tangible proof that the new life would be better.

"You have to remember that however she got there, she's at the top of the food chain as his mistress. She's untouchable. Turning her against him could get risky." She'd given them the school, but Mike hadn't seen anything else that would persuade Vanya to throw over Polzin. From the intel Claudia gathered, the woman had everything she needed with the apartment, the private driver, the club, and the not-too-frequent demands from Polzin.

"But his business is barbaric," Laurel said. "No woman should be forced to support that kind of life. She can't want to be in his organization."

"You're right," he agreed. "Though the right kind of domination can be fun."

"What a guy thing to say."

"I am a guy," he said. "But for the record, the first time I heard those words it was from a woman."

"Oh, that is... that's too much information," she said, waving her hand as if she could erase the words from the air.

"Be still," he snapped, covering her hands. "You could draw their attention."

She sucked in a breath. Due to his snapping orders or the chemistry that sizzled whenever they touched? No time to figure it out right now.

"You can let go," she said. "I'm still as a rock."

He removed his hand from hers slowly, telling himself it was all about avoiding detection rather than lingering over the sweet contact.

"Just keep your kink and quirks to yourself."

"Your loss," he said, putting his attention back on the school in the canyon below. Polzin was spending more time than Mike would've thought five women required. If he had cell service he'd notify Claudia so she could alert her contact at Interpol.

"I'm not a prude," Lauren clarified. "I know people get off on different things, but sex should be about mutual pleasure."

"Amen." Clearly, he'd brought up the wrong topic. The burning memory of that kiss was making him want things he couldn't have. That was how cases fell apart: one small mistake led to a distraction, then another mistake, and it snowballed until it consumed or crushed everything. He had to stop the cycle right here.

He cleared his throat, wishing it were as simple to clear his mind of the endless sensual possibilities with the woman stretched out beside him. It was all too easy to imagine a little domination-submission play with Lauren. He could show her the exquisite pleasure in either role. Just thinking about it made him hard again, but her resistance to the idea made him curious. Had Trinity or someone else in her past taken too much control in the bedroom?

Now wasn't the time to indulge his curiosity. Any pleasure he might eventually coax out of Lauren had to take a back seat to finding something to pin on Polzin. Her life depended on it.

As if on cue, the front door of the building opened and Polzin reappeared, Kozlov right behind him. Mike felt Lauren shiver. "Relax," he murmured. "This is progress." Everything indicated Kozlov carried the bulk of the workload in this area. While Polzin glowered at the men around him, he didn't direct any ire toward Kozlov specifically. Mike slipped the headphones over his ears and turned up the volume of his parabolic ear. He wanted to pick up and record as much of the conversation below as possible.

"Damn Trinity. We need a redhead," Andreas Polzin said. "One of tonight's party guests is partial. The others are most acceptable. Make sure they're ready for tonight's guests. And find me a damned redhead."

"It will be handled." Kozlov gave a nod to another man who immediately stalked toward the sedan.

"And where is Trinity's woman?"

Mike tensed. He glanced at Lauren, grateful she couldn't hear the conversation.

Kozlov shook his head. "There has been no sign of her."

Polzin scowled. "Remedy that. I won't have our endeavors here hampered. Trinity has done enough damage already."

"Yes, sir."

I won't let them find you, Mike vowed silently to Lauren. He watched Polzin disappear behind the dark glass of the limousine. Mike was sorely tempted to open fire just for the hell of it. He'd run across some people who stretched the definition of human, but Polzin won the prize.

"Mike!" She tapped his shoulder. "They're taking the women."

He shifted, watching the guards escort five women dressed in white t-shirts and black yoga pants into the two SUVs that had tailed the limousine. "Damn it." What the hell was Polzin's hurry? "Help me get down the license plate numbers. You take care of the SUVs. I'll get the limo and the sedan." He entered the info into the notepad of his phone as the vehicles drove away.

"Mike," Lauren urged.

"Hold on," he said. "There's only one way out of the canyon. If we move too soon they'll spot us."

LAUREN'S WORST-CASE scenario was playing out right in front of her and Mike barely twitched. They had to *do* something. Those women were in trouble, being taken to whatever came next in this heinous business. Awful as it was, her fear for the women in jeopardy forced Lauren to shake off the ice-cold dread of seeing the man who'd ordered Desmond's death as well as the man who'd carried it out. All that mattered just now was saving those women. Her connection to Desmond had dragged her into this and there was no turning back. She couldn't ignore what was happening and hope the police would get the job done.

She struggled to keep her word and obey Mike's order as the caravan rolled away. "We have to follow them." She braced herself for his argument. When he said nothing, she added, "You know I'm right."

When at last he stowed his gear, she breathed a sigh of relief. They eased back from the ridge, and then stood and raced for the car.

"Do you have a plan yet?" Lauren fastened her seatbelt.

"They said something about preparing the women

for a party. Tonight." He shifted the car into drive. "As soon as we get a signal, send the license plate numbers to Claudia."

"Okay." She did as he asked and waited for instructions. Her mind was whirling with ideas. If they could figure out where the party was being held maybe they could set up a sting—if it was the kind of party she suspected it would be.

The phone rang and Mike put it on speaker. "Where're they headed?" he asked Claudia.

"I picked up your caravan on the PCH headed for LA. You aren't far behind."

"Thanks, Claudia," Lauren said when Mike appeared absorbed with navigating traffic.

"Got you two covered," Claudia assured before ending the call.

A few minutes later on the Pacific Coast Highway, Mike slowed down. "There they are," he pointed, then slipped into another lane, using a truck to block their pursuit.

"About the party," she began, her mind already toying with how to get the women away from Polzin.

He cut her off. "One thing at a time, Nancy Drew."

"Hey, I consider that a compliment. She was a great character."

Mike shot her a raised eyebrow while staying a few cars behind the dark SUVs. "It wasn't meant as an insult. We just have to take care of one thing at a time."

"Right." She kept quiet, grateful when she was sure Polzin and his caravan were headed away from the coast. "I'm so glad they're not heading for the ports. I had visions of trying to find a container in a maze of identical containers."

"That's probably how some shipments are exported."

"They aren't shipments, they're women!" She covered her mouth, regretting her outburst. That behavior wouldn't give him any confidence in her ability to help him take down Polzin. Mike was right about that much. Saving the women would only be a start. They had to put an end to the school and this piece of Polzin's organization permanently. "Sorry."

"I understand."

He said it with such kindness she believed him. Those little glimpses under his tough, inscrutable exterior kept her looking for more. Conversations were like a scavenger hunt for his emotions. She wanted to fire back something upbeat, something courageous, but couldn't push the words past the lump in her throat. "I can't bear the thought of what might happen to them if we fail."

"We'll do all we can. Just remember that however this goes down, keeping *you* safe is my priority."

She could only nod. She didn't care that he hadn't said the words with any romantic or relationship intentions. He meant those words on a level that went beyond the fact that he was being paid to protect her. Of that she had no doubt. No one in her life had ever made such a heartfelt declaration. Desmond had cared about her, but mostly as it related to his interests. She had friends who loved her, friends she loved, but no one made her feel cherished the way Mike did. It was... significant. And strange considering they barely knew each other.

As Beverly Hills came into view she wrapped herself in the feelings swirling inside her. Protected, understood, valued. Empowered. This man—jaded or not—wouldn't let her down.

Whatever they were getting into, she promised herself she wouldn't let him down either.

CHAPTER 8

MIKE'S INSTINCTS were humming as they followed Polzin's caravan into the Hollywood Hills. "Do a search," he told Lauren. "Pull up Google Earth. Find out how many houses are on this street."

Lauren opened the app on the phone. "If we're stopped we can pretend we're looking for some star's home. I can name several who live in this neighborhood."

"That won't end well," he reminded her. "If anyone recognizes you it's over."

"I've decided to think positively." She dug for her sunglasses and put them on, flashing him a smile.

With the baseball cap, she might be any tourist with long blond hair studying a map. The SUVs slowed for a turn, drawing Mike's full attention back to them. As they turned into a private driveway, Mike cruised slowly past and captured as many details as possible. The SUVs had stopped at a big gate a short way up the long drive. Unable to see more, he kept going, following the curve of the road, but the neighborhood homes gave way to scrubby terrain and the only option was to make a turn.

"Check the map. Is there a place—higher ground —where we can watch what's going on in there?"

"I'm working on it," she said, focused on the screen.

"They must've brought the women in to entertain the buyers." He was thinking aloud as he drove past one luxurious estate after another. "They're short a redhead."

"I could be a redhead."

He glared at her. "No way." Turning down another street, he debated how to get a good view of the mansion. "I need to get eyes on Polzin."

"You think he'll just be lounging poolside?"

Mike shrugged. He didn't know what to think about much of anything right now. If anyone recognized Lauren, the police and the mob would descend on them like a tidal wave.

"You know it's the best way to get inside."

He shook his head. "We can't risk it. You're forgetting these men know you. Not just through Trinity's records, but you. Kozlov called you Lauren Marie."

That part had started to worry him. Why would

anyone in this crew fixate on an actress like her? She was gorgeous and talented, underrated to be sure. But she'd never traveled with Trinity. She'd never had an actual encounter with any of the Krushka syndicate until they killed Trinity. Why had they allowed her to get away? Sure they'd blown up her car, but he would bet his next paycheck there had been opportunities to take her out before she'd reached that motel. For some reason she was still alive. Possibly as a scapegoat for Trinity's murder. Or maybe one element wanted her dead while the other wanted her for something else. He had to keep Lauren off the grid until he learned who wanted what from her.

Mike found a place to park that gave them a sliver of a view of the mansion's opulent garden and what appeared to be a side entrance. He twisted around for the bag behind his seat and pulled out a pair of binoculars. The SUVs were parked in a circular driveway and the vehicles were positioned in a way that the women could be moved into the house with the least amount of exposure.

He used his phone to send the mansion's address to Claudia with a request for any ownership details.

"I can't believe this kind of thing goes on in this neighborhood," Lauren said.

"Claudia says Polzin is leasing," Mike explained when the response came through. "Apparently this property is managed by a real estate firm and used primarily for parties and events and the occasional movie."

"He's not getting away with this," she vowed quietly. "We can change things for those women. We can give them a second chance."

"Assuming they want one."

"No. You aren't taking me down that path again. We both saw those cells. They weren't there willingly. They're hostages."

He knew she was right, just as he knew this conversation would inevitably return to her idea of reaching out to Vanya again for help. He was torn between Lauren's admirable determination to make a difference and his obligation to keep her safe. No happy medium here. He'd never lost his perspective on a military or private operation before. As much as he wanted to analyze what made him feel differently about Lauren, he needed to focus on her case. Law enforcement agencies around the world wanted a piece of Polzin, but he'd slipped through every time they closed in. Mike wanted to take him down. Hard. Interrupting Polzin's operation would be a challenge, but unless they put the man in a prison or a grave, Lauren would never be safe.

"I reviewed everything Claudia found on the Krushka syndicate," he said. "Polzin values power and money, in that order. The closer we come to threatening those values, the bigger chance you end up dead. Or worse." He couldn't imagine what he'd do if

Polzin got control of Lauren. "We have to take this slow. Slow and smart."

"I'm not arguing with you," she insisted. "I'm just saying that someone has to step up. Let me talk to Vanya about the party. Between the two of us, I'm sure we can connect Polzin to Desmond's murder and to what they're doing at the finishing school. She can get me into that party tonight."

Vanya had given more than he'd expected with the tip on the school. They needed insider help if they had any chance at a rescue without casualties. "If we're reading her wrong, someone is likely to end up dead."

"I'm all ears if you have a better idea."

He didn't, that was the trouble. Unless he called Hank for an assist, which felt all wrong. The man was in town with his family and Mike wouldn't put them in Polzin's sites. Other than hanging Lauren out there as bait, a solution that could get her killed, he didn't have another way to flush out the bosses.

"We'll go back to the club," he said, starting the car. The idea burned a hole in his gut. "But you'll need a different disguise than last night and we'll need a cover story for me."

"Vanya won't talk if you're there."

"You can't go in alone," he protested. "We'll come up with another idea that gets me into that party." He didn't know what it would be, but he wouldn't put *her* in jeopardy.

"The obvious choice is posing as a potential buyer. You'll have to act."

"I'll manage." He understood Polzin's type and was familiar with the sort of men he associated with. "This isn't the first time I've gone up against bastards with unthinkable habits."

"The Angeles Forest killer?"

"Among others." His mind drifted back to that last SEAL mission. "So, where can we find clothing or costumes?"

"You're letting me decide?"

He nodded, reluctantly enchanted by her enthusiasm. "As long as it's not the soap studio or some trendy store at the mall."

Her soft laughter filled the car. "Back to Malibu." She reached for his phone and entered an address into his navigation app. "Nothing public, I promise."

"Someone you trust?"

"Absolutely." She held up her hand. "My friend will be the soul of discretion and her husband is about your size."

"Great." He'd be stuck in a stranger's clothes while she assumed yet another persona. He told himself it was a means to an end. Anything to get the job done. "Does your friend draw paparazzi?"

"That could be trouble," Lauren admitted. "I'll send a quick text and let her know we're on the way and that we need a clear path to her."

Mike hoped her friend was as trustworthy as Lauren believed.

JUST READING the friendly reply from her friend boosted Lauren's hope. Mike was quiet on the drive up the PCH. She couldn't guess what he was thinking, not with her mind whirling over what they'd found. Somehow they had to get into that party. Without evidence to call in the FBI or Interpol, their own ingenuity would have to do.

Lauren ordered herself to relax as they drove the last few miles. She lowered her window just enough to allow the breeze coming off the ocean to filter into the car. She inhaled deeply and closed her eyes. She imagined burying her toes into the sand and feeling the water rush over her feet and ankles. The car slowed and Lauren opened her eyes. She couldn't wait to see her friend.

"Zoe Langston?" Mike asked as he made the turn into the driveway. "How is this discreet?"

"She's my best friend. Are you a fan of her music?"

"By default. She's married to surf champion, Blake Scott."

Lauren wanted to pump her fist, happy she'd found something that might give her leverage for a compromise. "If you're nice I'll arrange an introduction and you can surf with him."

Mike laughed. "I'll just be over here holding my breath."

Lauren laughed, her first real one in days. "Pull to the left of the side driveway and we'll be out of range of any potential onlookers."

"Hope so."

On this side of the house, they were safe from prying eyes unless someone with a serious telephoto lens was out past the surf line in a boat. It had happened on rare occasions. Today, as Lauren gazed out over the private slice of beach, the waves were clear.

Zoe met them at the back door and pulled Lauren into a big hug. "What a relief it is to see you. I've been worried sick. Why didn't you call?"

Lauren felt a measure of the tension unravel under Zoe's unconditional support. "My phone was damaged," she explained with a sideways glance at Mike. She introduced him as the bodyguard who'd kept her safe and Zoe immediately embraced him as well, showering him with gratitude.

"Just doing my job," he replied.

Lauren shook her head. The man had no idea how to accept a compliment with any grace. She stepped in, sparing him any unnecessary conversation. "We need a favor."

"Anything." Zoe threw her arms wide. "Ask away."

Lauren smiled. "We need some formal-wear, makeup, and I need a wig."

"What's mine is yours." She looked Mike up and down. "Same goes for anyone keeping Lauren safe."

"Thanks," he said tightly.

"Don't worry," Zoe said. "You're built like my Blake. He's got a tux that will make the ladies swoon on sight."

Mike in a tuxedo was a mouthwatering image Lauren didn't need. "A tux is overkill for tonight," she replied. "I was thinking the charcoal pinstripe."

"Hmm…maybe." Zoe hummed, her gaze cruising over Mike. "Make yourself at home, honey. Lauren and I will see what we can come up with."

Mike gave a nod. "I have calls to make."

When Lauren and Zoe were alone in her bedroom, Lauren closed the door with a snap and leaned back against it. "I don't have a lot of time."

"What happened?" Zoe demanded, keeping her voice low. "And where did Mr. Hottie come from? He doesn't look like any security detail I've seen." She stepped in front of Lauren. "You don't get so much as a false eyelash until you spill."

"No time," Lauren protested. Mike would use every idle minute to come up with reasons to abort her idea to see Vanya again.

Zoe folded her arms, refusing to budge. "You're my best friend, Lauren. Tell me what's going on."

As quickly as possible, Lauren brought her up to speed about the murder and how they'd found signs that Desmond was making deals with criminals. She let Zoe's imagination fill in the blanks, leaving out details about the finishing school and the Russian mob. "No matter what you see or hear on the news I didn't kill Desmond."

"Of course you didn't," Zoe said with absolute faith as she stepped aside to give Lauren full access to her wardrobe. "Though you had plenty of reason to."

"Please don't say *that* in any interview."

"The police were already here and I've had a few calls from the press."

Lauren felt her chin drop. "I'm so sorry."

Zoe shrugged. "What's Hollywood without a little drama? It's not like I had to lie about not knowing anything."

"Mike explained that turning to my friends could make them accomplices or targets. Maybe both. I couldn't risk that. But no one followed us here. Mike made sure."

"Relax, doll. I've been watching the news and hoping you'd show up. I'm happy to do whatever I can. Let's help Mike find a suit first," Zoe said, wiggling her eyebrows.

"He's just the bodyguard. Don't get any ideas." Lauren didn't need any help on that front. She seemed to have new, enticing, and intimate ideas every time she looked at him.

"Too late," Zoe said cheerfully. "You deserve a hot fling. God knows Desmond had plenty. I wanted to wring his neck for treating you like crap."

"I let him do it," Lauren pointed out. "And I wasn't a complete doormat, despite public opinion."

Zoe gave her a quick hug. "I know."

They perused Zoe's husband's closet and emerged with two suits. They gathered ties, shirts, belts, and shoes and Zoe carried all of it out to Mike to try on in another room.

By the time she returned, Lauren had selected a few dresses, searching for just the right look. "Mike surfs and he's a huge fan of Blake's. Assuming we don't end up in prison," or dead, she didn't say, "do you think Blake would hit the waves with him one day?"

"Count on it."

"Tonight, in disguise," Lauren assured her friend, "we should get some proof to take to the police and clear my name and hopefully what we need to stop these monsters."

"Good." Zoe reached out and snagged an armful of dresses, carrying them to the dressing area. "Let's make a statement for whatever role you're playing tonight. What's Mike's favorite color?"

"Stop it," Lauren scolded gently. "I can't look like me anyway."

"So you do like him! How could you not? That body and..."

"Does your husband know you drool over strangers?"

Zoe laughed. "Blake has my undivided adoration

and loyalty and he knows it. You, however, are afraid of something."

Lauren shifted her attention to the dresses, trying to get into the head of a woman who would help a man buy and sell other women. "The police and a Russian mob are looking for me. Being afraid is a smart thing."

"That's not it," Zoe stated. "You're hung up on the hot bodyguard."

"He's so not my type."

"Please. He's every red-blooded hetero woman's type." Zoe held up one dress after the next, until she found a bold blue silk. "This is perfect. It matches his eyes."

"This is *not* a date," Lauren protested as she considered the dress. "I don't know. With a short black wig and contacts… brown or maybe green."

Zoe circled her finger in the air. "Only one way to know for sure. Off with your clothes."

Lauren stripped to her bra and panties and stepped into the dress. Zoe pulled the zipper up her spine and gave a low whistle. "Your backside looks great. Turn around."

"Yes, drill sergeant," Lauren teased.

Her friend only hummed a little as Lauren did the model's turn. "This has potential. With a black wig and smoky eye makeup no one will realize you're Lauren Marie Woods or Dr. Loveless."

"That's the goal." Lauren stepped to the mirror

and angled her body left and right. The dress clung to her curves, showing a generous amount of cleavage and her commitment to fitness. "This should keep the focus where it belongs."

"No one will be looking at your face, that's for sure."

Zoe helped her wriggle out of the dress and they gathered the right accessories. "I need one more dress. A step down from this one."

"No problem." They went through the selection and found a red dress that gave off a sexy power vibe without overdoing it. It would be perfect for her upcoming attempt to speak with Vanya.

"Stay for dinner," Zoe offered.

"We really can't." If she missed Vanya they'd have a real fight getting those women out of the mansion.

"A drink then. The stress is obvious, Lauren. Take a minute to catch your breath."

"The longer we stay the more risk it is for you." She was starting to sound like Mike.

"You didn't kill him. Surely there's a cop who will listen to your side."

"Leave it to Mike and me. We can handle this." She hoped. "You have no idea what Desmond was into." Lauren knew it would be years—if ever—before she could get the images of those captured women out of her mind. "Trust me, Zoe. I'll tell you the whole story as soon as I can."

Zoe studied her a bit too closely. "On one condition."

"What's that?" Lauren knew her friend trusted her unconditionally, though she might express more than a few doubts if she knew about the gang of human traffickers.

"Promise me you'll remember not all men are like Desmond."

Lauren rolled her eyes. "I know that."

"I wonder." Zoe tapped her foot. "Men like to give orders and they love to be right, but good men aren't selfish or mean. A good man, a man who truly cares has *your* best interests in mind."

"Well, if I'm not in prison or dead, I'll keep that in mind when I start dating again." She couldn't picture that yet. Dating felt too normal and far too risky. She wasn't sure how long it would take before she trusted her judgment of potential companions again.

"I say start with the man in front of you."

"Zoe, stop," Lauren pleaded. "Mike's not with me because he's interested. He's doing his job."

"Oh, he's interested," Zoe insisted. "If nothing else, consider him practice."

"Fine!" Agreeing with Zoe was the only way to get back to the task ahead of them. How had she not noticed how bossy her best friend was?

With a final hug, the borrowed clothing neatly packed and zipped into garment bags, she and Mike slipped away from the house and headed back to work.

"She worries about you," Mike observed.

"Yeah. She's a good friend." Lauren was relieved when he didn't press her for more details or another assurance that Zoe would keep the visit to herself.

"I grew up in California." His quiet statement surprised her. "Celebrities rarely impress me."

"Zoe isn't the norm," Lauren admitted.

"Neither are you," he said.

She wasn't sure how to reply.

"That's a compliment," he explained. "Say thank you."

"Thank you." She resisted the urge to ask him what prompted the compliment. Not with Zoe's have a fling speech disrupting her thoughts anyway. A fling with Mike would probably be life altering, but she couldn't grant herself that type of diversion. Not now.

"We should be able to catch Vanya at the club," she blurted. "I've been thinking about how to convince her to talk to us and then testify against Polzin."

"Big goals," he said. "You're assuming she knows something useful."

"She does." The more Lauren thought about it, the more she was certain this wasn't a case of wishful thinking, but solid fact. They just had to find the irrefutable link between Desmond and Polzin. "She's the ace up our sleeve."

Beside her Mike grunted, seemingly unconvinced, but he waited until they were back in the hotel suite to try and talk her out of this again. "Sending you in alone could backfire," he called from the other side of the bathroom door as she wriggled into the red dress she'd chosen to approach Vanya at the club.

"Of course you'd want to rehash this when I'm distracted." She glared at the door, hoping he heard the frustration in her voice.

"Look," he said. "I get the philosophy behind your approach. You want to appeal to her woman to woman, like the last time."

Ignoring him, Lauren tugged the short black wig into place and meticulously confirming no evidence of her natural blond hair remained. She started her makeup with the contacts that transformed her eyes from the distinct silver blue to a deep green. As she applied foundation and blush, Mike rattled on, hoping to change her mind. She wouldn't. Those women were her problem now. She didn't care if her determination was fueled by associative guilt.

Giving particular care to match her eyebrows to the wig color, she had everything on but the lip color and shoes when she stepped out of the bathroom.

Mike's jaw dropped. "You—"

She gave him her back. "Can you finish the zipper and hook please?"

His warm touch was fleeting and the only sound was the hushed rasp as the zipper came together.

"There you go."

She felt him step back, felt the absence of his body heat. Moving around him, she avoided eye contact as she slipped into the matching red heels Zoe recommended for this dress.

"You look…"

Mentally, Lauren filled in the blank with about a dozen likely adjectives before Mike finished the sentence.

"…exotic."

Lauren felt something like a blush warming her skin. No one had ever referred to her that way. Beautiful, sure. Lovely, sometimes. Occasionally she earned a 'striking'. Her personal favorite was 'girl-next-door pretty' when she was caught running errands without her makeup.

Then Mike scowled. "If Polzin sees you he could be a problem."

"He won't even be there," she said, dismissing his concern. "He's at the mansion overseeing the preparations for the party tonight, remember?"

Mike's dark eyebrows were still furrowed over his midnight-blue eyes. She walked over and caught his hand in hers, to hell with the temptation that touching him caused. "I'll be all right. No one will recognize me and I truly believe Vanya wants to help us."

One of those dark eyebrows arched. "I agree you don't look anything like Lauren Marie Woods."

She smiled. "Good."

His gaze dropped to her mouth and she remembered her lips were bare. She'd have to fix that before they left.

"Lauren."

"Yes?"

He tipped up her chin and captured her lips in a fierce kiss. Nothing tentative or seeking this time. Her heart skipped and her pulse leaped straight to all-out need. Something inside her sighed as his tongue plunged and retreated with bold, sensual promise. Fingers digging into the firm muscles of his shoulders, she let her head fall back, reveled in the soft scrape of his short whiskers against her skin. He rained kisses down the column of her throat and followed the slope of her collarbone with tantalizing nips.

"You taste like Lauren," he breathed against her ear.

She would've laughed, but he pulled her close and she felt his erection against her belly. The words in her head now had little to do with Zoe's advice. She wanted Mike. Now. Here. She pushed at his shirt, pulling the hem from his waistband and sliding her palms across rippling abs and up over hard planes of his sculpted back.

He cupped her backside and boosted her up and she wrapped her legs around his lean waist, rocking her hips against him. It was a wonder their clothing didn't burn away.

"Mike," she whispered, with more need than she'd ever felt for another man. His hands roamed along her thighs, trailed up and teased her breasts through the fabric, and then back down to trace the narrow outline of the cheeky panties she wore. Each place he touched turned molten, desperate for more.

For him.

The fires he lit burned away all rational thought until all she felt was the sweet-hot need. She reached down and stroked the length of him through his jeans. His responsive groan gave her a delicious sense of power. She stroked again. And once more. He felt enormous. Virile. Alive. She wanted to feel all of that, all of *him* deep, deep inside her.

She stilled. Was this his attempt to distract her? With monumental effort, she flattened her hands against his chest and drew away from that hungry mouth of his. "We can't do this now." Later, yes. *Definitely* later.

"Sorry." He shook his head. "My fault." He set her on her feet, his hands lingering on her hips while she found her balance. "I crossed the line."

"Not alone." She smiled, her lips feeling puffy and full—in the best possible way. She leaned around him to check the time. "We'd better get going if we hope to catch Vanya. If she's on tonight's guest list we don't have a lot of time."

Mike didn't offer a dissenting opinion as he straightened his clothes and pulled on a leather jacket.

Using the mirror by the door, she smoothed her clothing and finished her disguise with a sassy red lip stain. The effect made her eyes stand out. Mesmerizing green eyes that bore no resemblance to the woman the cops and half of LA and Hollywood were searching for.

Mike said she tasted the same and he would know, but she didn't feel like the same woman who'd allowed Desmond to dictate her life for years. No matter what happened with Vanya or Polzin, she'd never be that woman again. Her transformation may have started hours before Desmond's murder, but after this short acquaintance with Mike she was absorbing his influence as well. Tiny steps taking her closer to the woman she wanted to be.

A woman who knew her heart, spoke her mind, and made the right moves off camera—where it mattered most.

CHAPTER 9

MIKE CONSIDERED it a small miracle they returned to the seedy club with their clothing still intact. The sizzling chemistry was indisputable and as much as he wanted to capitalize, to indulge both of them, this wasn't the time.

She'd spent years in what he'd determined had been a relationship based on little more than mutual neglect. He gave her credit for holding up, but this wasn't the time for distractions. For either of them. He'd leaped right past attracted and protective when he looked at her in that red dress. He was feeling outright possessive. More so with every passing hour. The dress treated the public to an excellent view of her luscious curves, but not quite enough to satisfy him. Of course, judging by his persistent hard-on for her, anything shy of nude wouldn't be enough for him.

"I'll be fine," she'd said when he dropped her off at the curb like some lackey.

A profound reply eluded him. Instead, he played his role as her driver. No matter how strong and determined she appeared, Mike was increasingly uncomfortable with her going in alone. Even with Claudia monitoring the situation, if Lauren were caught, if her talk with Vanya made Kozlov or one of his cronies suspicious, Mike would have his hands full rescuing her. He wasn't worried about Kozlov killing her in public. The bastard wasn't a fool. Still, the situation was way too dicey for Mike's comfort. He knew it was his issue and he owned it. Her disguise was effective, but to him, no matter the wig or contacts or heavy layers of makeup, she was always Lauren.

It was the strangest thing. Inexplicable. He couldn't make the realization fit into the context of the last time a group of women needed to be rescued. Standing guard alone gave him too much time to analyze it. He called Claudia. "Did you trace the ownership of the Royal?"

"It's a dive Polzin uses to launder money," she replied.

Mike struggled for the detached calm he normally employed during a case. "I want to know if or how Trinity was connected. Gut instinct." Trinity was dead, but something was wrong if the police weren't finding ties to the Krushka syndicate right here in East Hollywood.

"Public records say it belongs to Tri-Star Enterprises."

"Bingo." Mike knew it. Tri-Star was one of Trinity's companies.

"Looks like he owns a couple of other clubs in the area."

Claudia went on but Mike's gut tightened more with each passing second. Having Lauren wear any sort of wire had been too big a risk. The only eyes they had on her were Claudia's. She'd hacked into the club's security system and was watching via the establishment's own cameras. He shook his head. He never should've let Lauren out of sight. Any one of Kozlov's men could be in there watching for her. Vanya could have ratted her out by now. They'd left Polzin at the mansion, but that didn't mean he'd stayed there. What was Mike doing, letting Lauren walk into the lion's den alone?

"This was a mistake. I'm going in," he said.

"Stay put," Claudia ordered. "Everyone inside looks happy enough."

"Let me see. Send it through."

"You don't trust me?"

The question was a trap and he knew it. "It's my job to keep her safe."

"Then why'd you let her go in?"

Because she'd insisted. He could hardly admit that

to Claudia, though she'd likely reached that conclusion on her own. Nothing resembling a valid excuse came to mind, so he blurted out Lauren's logic. "She's working a woman-to-woman approach. She thinks Trinity might've been trying to save Vanya."

"She's smart. If you go in, you'll wreck everything. A man like you sniffing around Polzin's mistress would bring an army of Russian thugs down on you."

"Maybe that's the better play," Mike said, thinking aloud.

"Hardly. You're good, but solo against all of them? No way. Besides, if I didn't know what Lauren was wearing, I couldn't even spot her."

"That's good to hear." He hoped Claudia wasn't just yanking his chain about the effectiveness of Lauren's disguise. Either way, it was done now. If Lauren was working, he needed to do the same. "Have you found a money trail? Trinity was too greedy to be part of this or take these risks for free."

It bothered Mike that so many of the missing women were last seen with Trinity and yet the police hadn't seemed to notice. Those women had families who deserved answers. Polzin had the means and will to apply unbearable pressure whenever and wherever it was required. Did he own more people in the police department other than Treadwell? Higher up the chain of command maybe? Mike felt confident that question had already been answered when

Kozlov showed up at that faked meeting with an attorney.

The thought made him twitchy. Picking up his cell, he sent Lauren a text, requesting verification of her progress. "Did you spot her yet?" he asked Claudia.

"Yeah, I have her now but I had to look really close at every female face in the joint. She's doing great. That red dress is killer," Claudia said, a hint of laughter in her voice. "If I didn't know you better, I'd say you have a little crush on our red-carpet client."

"Come on, now," he countered, trying to match her light tone. "You're the only girl for me no matter how inaccessible you are."

"Inaccessible?" She snorted. "That sounds about right for you, Mr. Distant."

He laughed and was starting to relax when a big black car pulled up. Kozlov and his muscle Maksimov got out and Mike's blood ran cold. He gave the information to Claudia, but he braced for action. "Where is Lauren?"

"She's chatting with Vanya. Ah... they just went through a door behind the bar."

Mike shifted in the seat. "Do you have a visual on her?"

"Wait... *wait*... I do now. They're in a dressing room, still talking. I'm a master at multi-tasking, but searching financials, keeping an eye on the cameras, and distracting you appears to max me out."

Mike breathed a sigh of relief. "Don't worry, I won't tell anyone that your super powers have limits." Not that he had anyone to tell. The Guardian Agency was more compartmentalized than the Pentagon. Following the press conference when the sheriff accepted all the praise for capturing the Angeles Forest killer, there'd been an attorney with an offer and a contract waiting on his doorstep. Once Mike had signed his name, he'd received a phone programmed with Claudia's number. Since that first day the system worked perfectly for him. The agency paid him on time, he got to surf every morning when he wasn't on a case, and he could take pride in his work again.

"I need to follow a few leads," Claudia said. "Can I trust you to stay put?"

"As long as you've got eyes on Lauren."

"She's safe. Trust me. Charging in will change that," Claudia warned.

Mike watched the street. This part of town would never meet the criteria for safe. But was anywhere safe enough for Lauren? A Russian syndicate boss had established himself in a mansion in Beverly Hills and the man's mistress was meeting with the only woman who could unravel the operation.

"I'll behave," he agreed reluctantly.

Claudia must have heard his teeth grinding. "Too bad I'm not there to see that in person."

MIKE

"I won't move until I get the signal," he promised. Though it wouldn't be easy.

"Good." She disconnected, leaving Mike alone with his thoughts again.

The silence that pressed in on him wasn't remotely comfortable.

Vanya's dressing room was small, but well-appointed with an antique vanity, a plush sofa upholstered in mauve velvet, and matching slipper chair. Lauren sank into the chair. "Thank you for taking the time to speak with me."

The rest of her plea for help simply dissolved. She hadn't forgotten her lines in years, but now, when it mattered most, she was tongue-tied. When Vanya had asked her name, Lauren had given her the name she and Mike had decided on, Renae Ford. So far, so good.

When Vanya said nothing, Lauren ventured, "After the way I behaved the last time we met, I was afraid you wouldn't want to—"

Vanya wheeled around. "Don't try to fool me. I know who you are. You are Desmond's woman."

"I—I…" Lauren couldn't spit out an effective response as her mind spun in frantic circles. Vanya only needed to say the word and Lauren would be caught. Mike had been right all along that this plan would get her killed. She hoped it wouldn't get him killed as well. Her throat tightened.

"Do not worry." Vanya perched on the padded stool in front of the vanity. "The others will be fooled." She crossed her legs and stared at Lauren. "You found the school, yes? Speak freely, there is only a camera watching this room, no listening devices. Andreas likes me to be watched at all times but my chatter bores him."

Lauren dared to breathe. "We found it. The women were moved this morning."

"I know this."

"What will happen to them?"

"Tonight?" Vanya met her gaze. "Nothing bad. They are… samples?" she said as if unsure of the proper word.

Mike's gut had been right. Tonight was about showing off the women as merchandise. Lauren's stomach clenched, but she kept the reaction off her face.

"After tonight… I do not know," Vanya added quietly.

Lauren leaned forward. "Get me into that party," she murmured. "As Renae Ford, I can be a new buyer. I'll get the women out."

Vanya shook her head. "This is not a good idea. Andreas deals only with men. He will kill you. And me if he learns I help you."

Lauren sat back once more, changing her tactics.

"You told the police I was in the office when Desmond was shot."

"It was required of me." Vanya got up and crossed to a small cabinet on the opposite side of the room. Pulling out a bottle of vodka, she splashed some into a glass. "Lie or die." She held her hands like a balance scale raising one, then the other. "There are no good choices."

Lauren considered what she thought she'd known about Desmond, comparing that to his final moments of life. Then she put it in the context of this horrible human trafficking organization. Maybe that night in his office really had been more than just another tryst with the wrong woman.

"You want drink?" Vanya held up her glass.

Lauren shook her head and ventured, "You want out." She sensed it must be true. Polzin would tire of her eventually. It was likely old mistresses were killed without remorse to control information leaks and expenses. There was no other reason for Vanya to reveal the school. She had to know her days were limited. "Desmond gave you an exit strategy."

"You are wrong. I was a test for Desmond." Vanya raised her glass. "He failed."

Lauren didn't believe her. "That may have been how it started. Tell me when it changed."

Vanya sipped at the vodka, her lipstick leaving a hot pink imprint on the crystal. "Your man was not so innocent in this."

"I'm well aware of his faults." They didn't have hard evidence of his association with Polzin, but she knew 'her man' had been up to his eyeballs in this disaster. "He tried to help you, didn't he?"

"You should go." Vanya returned to the seat in front of the vanity. "Go far away. Andreas is too strong, his organization is too perfect now."

Not so perfect if Desmond stopped sending women to the school. "I don't care," Lauren blurted. "I will help those women. Tonight." In trying to help Vanya, Desmond had possibly done something decent, though it had killed him.

"What can you do?" Vanya set the glass on her dressing table. "We are only women. Our traps are different, yes, but we are caught just the same."

The cynicism, the fatalistic outlook wasn't surprising considering everything Vanya must have seen through the years. Lauren had to find a way to crack through that shell and appeal to the woman inside. "You could make a difference," Lauren said. "I'm not working alone. With your help we can save those women."

Vanya dismissed the idea with a flick of her fingers. "Five women? What difference does that make?"

Quite a big difference for the women involved, Lauren thought, but that wasn't the right answer. "Five women and you," Lauren said pointedly. "You could be free. Your assistance would shut down

Polzin. He and Kozlov and all the others would go to prison."

"He prefers to kill me."

"He can't if he's behind bars."

Vanya's laughter sounded brittle. "You do not know Andreas Polzin."

The party would start in just a few hours. Desperate, Lauren tried again. "Introduce me. That's all. Get my buyer and me into the party and we'll do the rest."

"You do not know him," Vanya repeated sadly.

"Well, you don't know my new man," Lauren countered. "If you won't help, don't get in the way."

"This is big talk for an actress." Vanya turned back to her mirror, studying her face. She caught Lauren's gaze in the reflection. "We are not in a movie. If you try this you are in real danger with real guns and bullets."

"We have a plan. Better than Desmond's," Lauren said. "What do you have to lose?"

Vanya tapped her black-tipped fingernail to the marble vanity top, and then she shrugged. "I suppose we all must die eventually."

A sharp knock sounded as the dressing room door swung open, revealing Andreas Polzin. Lauren's heart nearly stopped.

Polzin's expression turned from stone to thunderous when he realized his mistress was not alone. Then he leered at her. "What is this?"

CHAPTER 10

LAUREN'S THROAT went dry as she stood. Had Vanya lied about only having a camera in here? What would she do? Polzin stalked closer, his eyes traveling over Lauren's body from head to toe. She'd met powerful men, but this one didn't bother to hide his rapacious nature. He wore authority like a crown, the ultimate ruler of his domain.

Mike's warnings echoed in Lauren's head. She was doomed and he was too far away to intervene. Surely the head of the Krushka syndicate would recognize her. If not her face, then he'd sense her fear or hear her knees knocking.

Vanya rose gracefully, moving toward him as naturally as a moth to flame. "How fortunate that you are early today, my love."

"Fortunate?" One dark eyebrow dipped low over his eye.

"Yes." Vanya slid her hand up and down his arm. "For both of us." She kept Polzin in the middle of the small room. "May I introduce Renae Ford? She asked to meet you."

"Why?" Polzin's gaze narrowed as he raked Lauren from head to toe once more.

Lauren gathered the role of buyer's assistant close about her, burrowing into the part as though it were the warmest of coats on a frigid night. "My employer is diversifying his investments with a new venture. This requires a certain type of stock. You have a reputation for supplying the best."

"Buyers come to me. Not their whores."

Lauren held his hard gaze. "Yet, here I am."

"You are a woman." His lip curled in derision. "I deal only with men."

Her heart raced, but she couldn't be the first to blink. "A fact we understand. But would you deal with a man you met here?" She spread her hands to indicate the private quarters of his mistress.

"Swiftly, I assure you," Polzin replied.

Lauren gave a light laugh, despite the image of Desmond's lifeless body flashing through her mind. "Vanya said the same. She is incredibly lucky to be yours. I was very intrigued by her. She's a beautiful dancer."

"She is," he agreed, accepting the drink Vanya served him.

"Our venture doesn't infringe or compete with your establishments," Lauren continued.

"How can you be so sure?" he asked.

"How could any wise businessman not?" According to Mike and Claudia no one had successfully chipped away at any Krushka territory. None had held when Polzin wanted to expand either.

The mob boss settled on the sofa with his drink and pointed to the cushion, signaling for Vanya to join him. "What is it you want?"

"Simply an invitation to further discussion."

He gestured for her to continue.

"The terms and such are not mine to discuss. I manage the inventory once it's acquired," she explained. She wanted to push harder, but any misstep and this meeting would blow up in her face. Polzin needed to see her as an assistant. She could be confident, but she had to respect the ironclad boundaries.

"You are American. How do you know my Vanya?"

She gave him a secretive smile. "Women know women," she demurred. She couldn't mention Desmond. Giving him any context to recognize her would be too much risk.

Polzin turned to Vanya. "You vouch for her?"

Vanya nodded. "I like her."

"Hmm." He snapped his fingers. "Fetch her phone and her bag."

Lauren managed to keep her hands from shaking as she handed her purse to Vanya. The woman carried it to Polzin with a smile that managed to be sexy and content simultaneously. From the moment Polzin had arrived, all signs of the jaded cynic had evaporated and only a devoted lover remained.

Of all the actresses in Hollywood, Lauren ranked Vanya as the most talented.

Lauren couldn't imagine this kind of life. No control or say in even the smallest things. Vanya might be doing what she loved each night as she danced on that stage, protected and safe from poverty or harm, but the price was astronomical.

Both women waited in silence as Polzin searched Lauren's purse and then scrolled through her phone, his sharp mind surely noting contacts and numbers. Trusting Mike, Lauren by default trusted Claudia to provide a background that would hold up to even Polzin's scrutiny.

With a satisfied grunt, he returned the phone and purse through Vanya. "Now, take off your clothes."

Lauren blinked. "Pardon me?"

Polzin shrugged. "If you're wearing a wire, you will die. Here and now."

Vanya's eyes rounded before she regained control.

"As you wish." Slowly, and with remarkable detachment, she undressed. If the man got the slightest hint she was wearing a wig, it was over. When she'd removed everything but her bra and panties, she held out her arms. "Would you like a closer inspection?"

He nodded to Vanya.

Vanya stood. She moved toward Lauren. Lauren held her breath. Her fingers icy, Vanya unhooked Lauren's bra and removed it. Her small, cool hands moved over and under Lauren's breasts. It was all Lauren could do to remain still. Vanya's hands moved down her body, smoothing over her bottom, between her legs and, lastly, sliding her fingers around the waistband of her skimpy panties. Lauren didn't breathe again until Vanya turned to Polzin.

"No wire."

Polzin surveyed Lauren's body. "Very well. You have earned the invitation your boss requires. Fortunately, your request is well-timed. We are hosting a buyer's show tonight. You will receive the details shortly. Now, leave us."

Lauren made a production of dressing, taking her time. Polzin ordered Vanya to turn off the camera. She did as he asked and returned to his side.

"It's been a pleasure." Lauren smiled broadly as she headed for the door.

Polzin watched her go. Vanya was already on her knees in front of him.

Lauren's body sagged with relief when she was out of the dressing room and clear of the security detail in the hallway. Surrounded by the garish lights and sounds as well as the push of the club patrons, it was a challenge to keep her composure. She counted her steps until she reached the brisk air of the December evening. With a deep breath, she relished the sanctuary of knowing Mike's eyes were on her again. She wanted a long, sanitizing shower after being so close to the slimy Polzin. One shower might not be enough, she thought, as the extravagant Lotus sports car Claudia had arranged stopped at the curb.

The passenger window rolled down and Mike leaned over. "Get in."

She hurried to comply—not because they were certainly under surveillance or she was eager to please him. She just wanted out of here. Fast. How could one man's order sound like comfort and security while another man's order evoked dread and resistance?

"We have the invitation," she said as he left the club behind.

"You okay?"

For the first time since she'd convinced him to look for Vanya she felt like they were in too deep. "I don't know anymore."

"Staying put was one of the hardest things I've ever had to do." He stopped for a traffic light. "Claudia threatened to send a team in to take me out if I moved."

The idea almost made Lauren laugh. Almost. "Polzin," she began. Just saying his name sent a chill down her spine. "He's expecting us tonight." The cell in her purse chirped and she jumped. Checking it, another shiver rippled through her. "Directions to the mansion where they took the women." She expelled a big breath. "We're in."

"We might just have a tail, too," he said, his eyes on the rearview mirror. "So Vanya is cooperating?"

Lauren cleared the nerves from her throat. "Yes."

"That's not an overwhelming endorsement."

"She could've told him the truth when he walked in and she didn't. She's on our side."

Mike's fingers flexed on the steering wheel. "He could've killed you without a second thought."

She was well aware. Maybe one day she'd get past this residual, hair-raising sensation that she'd made a narrow escape. "He didn't. I'll admit that I'm seriously creeped out after the encounter, but I'm not backing down."

Mike met her gaze, something like admiration glinted in his deep blue eyes. "I'm with you all the way."

HER USE of us and we was his biggest problem with this entire mess, Mike decided as he let the tail follow them back to the hotel. He couldn't get into the party without her but his every instinct nagged him to keep her far from Polzin and his crew. When Claudia had reported Polzin's unexpected entrance and what he'd forced Lauren to do in that dressing room, Mike had almost come apart. The only thing that kept him in the damned car was the realization that one wrong move would mean Lauren's death.

"You did a good job," he admitted. "But walking into the lion's den twice in one night is pushing our luck. It's a bad idea."

"Don't start that again." She tugged the seatbelt and fidgeted in her seat. "Neither of us can get those women out alone. He won't do business with a woman."

No, but there had to be a way to avoid putting her close to Polzin or the men who'd murdered. She had the invitation. They'd been by the mansion. He could take another look and create a sniper-style attack to clear a path. It was the sort of plan that sounded good in theory. As a sniper, he'd be too far away to pose as her boss or to help if something went wrong. That sort of effort required backup for a successful, casualty-free rescue. There was no time. Claudia was a good start but outmaneuvering Polzin during his party would be thorny. Tonight would test Mike's creative problem solving skills more than ever.

It was time to call in a favor. Maybe two.

At the hotel, he parked the car and cut the engine, but he stayed put. Their tail parked across the lot. Two men, apparently sent to watch. Somewhere in the city one or more of Polzin's other men were searching for the right redhead for tonight's preview.

Their callous disregard for women, the lack of humanity, made him want to punch something.

"Are we going in?" she asked.

"Yes." They had to go back into that luxurious suite that was far too small for his comfort. "What did you tell him about us? About me?" It sounded better when he rephrased it.

She released her seatbelt with a click. "Just what we discussed. I gave him what he needed to hear." Her eyes flashed with humor. "I even said you're my employer, which makes you my boss."

He'd like to be. The thought filled his brain, followed by a parade of visions of her submitting to his erotic demands.

Why in the hell couldn't he shake that unfortunate conversation? He never should've brought up the subject of sex games. Teasing her wasn't a valid explanation. Neither was testing her reactions. He had better control than that in and out of the bedroom. He was on a case here.

The truth was, each revelation about her ex gave him the impression Trinity had been selfish in every area of his life. He'd kept a tight leash on Lauren's career because it lined his pockets. He'd kept a tighter leash on her personal life because it boosted his status and respectability to date fan-favorite Dr. Loveless. He didn't have to worry about her cheating on him or even leaving him, she was too classy for that. Bastard. And it drove Mike crazy just thinking about it… about how the man had neglected her and used her.

She might not see herself as a top A-lister in town, but her poise in the media, her good reputation on the set, gave her more clout than she realized. People saw her as the working-class girl who made it, the woman in control, and exactly where she wanted to be. It might not be true, but Lauren didn't let the public close enough to bust the myth. Why had she allowed Mike to see what she hid from others? Not everything she'd shared was essential to her case. Why did that make him want to reciprocate? Why did it make him want her so?

"Polzin will assume we're lovers," he said, his throat dry as hell. At his statement, her eyes went wide and her lips parted. Her hand froze on the door handle. He sympathized with the reaction. His mind had shot right back to the excellent kisses as well.

"Of course," she said after a moment. "I'll keep that in mind tonight. To him, women are playthings or tools to use."

"That's not what's happening here." He scrubbed at his face and yanked the key out of the ignition. "Inside." He couldn't stay out here, pretending to be a man he didn't want to be with a woman he wanted too much.

He walked beside her, but he kept his hands and lips to himself. If he kissed her now, it wouldn't be about control or business. He couldn't risk her life on the slim chance the men watching them recognized the personal attachment he was feeling. Once they were safe in the suite, Lauren set to work like a costume designer possessed. He was grateful for the distraction and limited conversation as she focused on presentation and he made the calls that would smooth the way for their escape.

He checked in with Claudia and together they studied the blueprints of the mansion. So far she hadn't come across a report of a missing redhead, but adults weren't considered missing until at least twenty-four hours had passed. By then it would be too late. Polzin would insist on someone beautiful and clean to fill out the preview roster tonight. Mike was determined to keep another woman out of the snare. Rescuing five plus Lauren and Vanya would be tough but he intended to get the job done with no casualties.

His mind turned it over and over as he dressed, thinking of the so-called finishing school and the clubs they'd waded through. "I'm an idiot," he said aloud, checking his watch. No matter where they picked up the redhead, they were taking her to one place: the party at the mansion. If they hurried they could ambush the kidnapper on the road. "Can we leave ASAP?"

"Sure," Lauren replied. "My makeup's done," she added one final touch, "now."

"Damn it," he muttered, fumbling with the knot of

his tie. A sniper attack didn't require this nonsense. He suddenly wished he'd insisted on a different approach tonight.

"Having performance issues, dear?"

"What?" Mike loosened the knot and started over. He didn't want to spend the night among Polzin and his sharks with a convenient noose around his neck.

"You're twitching like an understudy called up on reviewer night."

He caught a glimpse of her in the mirror, then forced his attention on adjusting the silk at his throat. "I don't want to know what that means."

"It's a stage thing that means you look nervous." She paused, securing a glittering golden earring that dripped nearly to her shoulder. "Whoa," she said, her eyes on his tie. "That's a four-in-hand."

"What?"

"The knot." She crooked a finger. "It's wrong. Come here."

His feet were rooted to the floor. Moving wasn't an option. It would put him closer to her and worse, too close to the bed. Minefields weren't as dangerous as staying in this room with her. "It's tied, isn't it?"

"Yes." She made an impatient sound. Crossing the room, the deep blue fabric of her dress shimmered, taunting him with all the curves he couldn't touch. "Polzin and the others will expect a full Windsor knot."

"How can you possibly know that?" He leaned

back, but her fingers were already loosening the tie. He forced himself to stay put. "It's a tie. Guys don't care."

"Maybe guys don't care, but these men will. I met Polzin today, remember? And I've met men like him —sans the illegal activities—since diving into this industry."

As if he could forget she'd stripped for the SOB. He warred with the urge to dodge her hands, or move them to the places where his body craved her touch. He had a feeling that it would be damned hard not to knock Polzin senseless the first time he looked at Lauren tonight.

"The tie underscores your background."

"Bull."

She shrugged a shoulder. "A four-in-hand isn't right for your build." The length of silk slid back and forth under his collar as she adjusted the ends to her liking. Then she stopped, her hands resting lightly on his chest.

Could she feel his heart hammering? Using the tie like a blindfold would be more fun—for both of them. Somehow he kept the words in his head as his gaze fell to her mouth. He wanted another taste of her soft lips warming to his kiss, but they'd already had one near miss. Finding his last ounce of restraint, he backed out of her reach. "My way is fine."

She seemed to snap out of her trance. "It's not." She tugged again, her gaze intent as she looped, twisted, and snugged until the knot at his throat satisfied her. "The man you're playing tonight has more money than Bill Gates. His tailor wouldn't allow him to ruin his image with the wrong knot." She turned him to the mirror. "See the difference?"

He did. "No." In the reflection he caught the quick, exasperated roll of her eyes.

"Polzin will see it, that's the point."

He grunted, which was as much of an answer as she was going to get.

"I like the earring," she teased.

Claudia had couriered over a very special platinum earring for him to wear. The jeweled eyes of the gargoyle were actually the latest in miniature audio and video transmitting equipment. Claudia would be recording every minute of tonight.

"I'm more worried he'll see you." Despite the wig and makeup, Mike saw Lauren Marie Woods, popular actress. Not even the contacts that turned her eyes to an impossible emerald green fooled him. "We need to rethink this."

"No." The straight, black hair brushed her chin as she shook her head. "Vanya risked too much for us to bail out."

"I don't mean bail, I mean rethink it."

She planted her hands on her hips. "You don't believe I can handle it."

"That's not it." Well, not all of it. He could hardly explain it to her when he didn't have the vocabulary to define this thing inside him that went beyond basic attraction. The body and face were outstanding, but the fascinating woman under the gloss and polish had him in a twist.

Lauren had exhibited courage his fellow SEALs would admire. When he'd opened this case he hadn't expected her to care about anything other than saving her skin. It was a rare day when he was proved wrong. He didn't know how to admit it.

"You know what?" she snapped. "I'm not sure I can count on you." She plucked her small purse from the bed and checked the contents as she headed for the door. "Stay here. I've memorized Officer Cooper's phone number if I need backup."

"Wait." He caught her elbow as she stomped past him. "Just wait a minute," he repeated. She couldn't call Cooper. Not yet. The words he needed to say were more difficult when she didn't look like herself, but he studied the woman under the disguise.

"Make it quick." She stopped, but didn't turn around. "If we're late, we could be locked out."

"You'll be great." Several lives, theirs included, were riding on her ability to perform as a buyer's assistant. All he had to do was act the part of a cold, wealthy man with a general disregard for women as anything beyond useful servants. Thanks to Lauren's ability to costume him, his job was more than halfway done. "You can count on me. I'll play the part and I'll have the exit route ready."

"If I thought waiting would work, I'd agree to hide until the authorities rounded up Polzin and his syndicate." She stared up at him, her face imploring. "Frankly, I'm not so sure they're even looking for these guys."

"I know." He believed she'd prefer to execute a rescue that wouldn't drum up media attention, but he'd learned she wasn't shy when she thought she could accomplish something. That same core belief had carried her away from home and set her on a successful path in one of the most unforgiving industries. "And you're right. We need to strike now while Polzin is in town."

She nodded. "Thank you. Bringing Desmond's killer to justice and rescuing those women isn't enough. We need to… cut off the head of the snake."

He grinned and picked up the keys to the car. "You got it, baby."

CHAPTER 11

Hollywood Hills, 7:45 p.m.

THE LOTUS FLOATED through traffic as they headed out to the mansion for the party. He lost the tail when they stopped for drinks at a swanky bar, and managed to maintain just enough lead time to park the car out of sight along the drive to the mansion.

"What if the driver won't stop?" Lauren's show of nerves somehow settled his own. "This could be the wrong move."

Claudia had been monitoring the police bands. An abduction of a young woman with red hair had been reported in West Hollywood by the victim's roommate. A quick check of traffic cams and Claudia had spotted the black sedan from the finishing school in the area. With the windows tinted she couldn't confirm the redhead was in the car, but it was definitely headed this way.

"Trust me." Mike flashed Lauren a smile. "I'm very good at this part."

"We'll get them all out, right?"

"We will. Now, sit tight while I do this. I'll be back before you know it."

"But—"

"Trust me," he repeated.

"Right." Her tight smile didn't quite reach her eyes. "Be careful. That's an order."

"Aye, aye, captain," he replied with a wink.

As he strolled back down the road, the tie pinched and the shoes chafed. He preferred his tactical gear for a reason. Distracting himself from the minor irritations, he thought about how to play this. By now, his face and fake name were on the guest list next to Lauren's alias. The information had been requested by Polzin's people via Lauren's cell. No matter that everything was set, Mike had no more than a few seconds of surprise on his side for this next move.

He crouched low, creeping closer to the last possible ambush point out of view of the sentry stationed at the entrance gate to the long drive. Then he waited for the man assigned to the kidnapping task. People who disappointed Polzin didn't have long life spans. If the boss wanted a redhead, Mike knew the man would deliver one.

As the minutes ticked by, he thought maybe he'd

underestimated the efficiency of the crew. He set a timer on his watch for the drop-dead moment he had to abandon this idea. He and Lauren had to arrive along with the other buyers or Polzin would be suspicious.

Finally headlights came into view. When he'd confirmed it was the right car, Mike stepped out into the road and waved.

The car rocked to a stop less than a yard from Mike's knees. "Get out of the way," the driver shouted.

"Can you give me a ride to the party? I have a flat tire."

The driver looked around. "Where's your car?"

Mike jerked a thumb up the road. "Next curve. I pulled to the shoulder, but it's narrow and I didn't want it to get dinged." He shrugged. "I couldn't exactly call Triple A and expect the guard at the gate to allow them in."

The driver's gaze narrowed. "You are alone?"

"My assistant's guarding the car," Mike said. "How about a lift? These shoes aren't made for hiking and I don't think Mr. Polzin will be happy if we're late."

"Get in." Clearly the driver knew better than to refuse one of the guests.

"Great, thanks." Mike opened the passenger door to an empty car. He worried he'd made a mistake until he heard a whimper from the shadows of the back seat. He couldn't see the woman but the noise sounded female. "What's her problem?" he asked as he dropped into the seat.

"She gets car sick." The driver put the sedan in gear and started up the road.

"I guess this is her lucky day." Mike plowed a fist into the driver's ear, and then clotheslined him. While the driver struggled to breathe, Mike jerked the steering wheel, pulling the car to the shoulder. The driver tried to accelerate, but Mike knocked the gearshift to neutral. He applied the necessary pressure to just the right point and the driver was down for the count.

"Can you drive?" Mike asked the girl as he slammed the gearshift into Park.

"Y-yes."

Mike shoved the driver out onto the road and performed a quick three-point turn until the car was aimed away from the mansion. "Do you know where the nearest police station is?"

Standing on shaky legs, she nodded. "I'll find it."

"Good. Go straight there." He hauled the unconscious driver into the trunk and used the jerk's tie to hogtie his hands and feet behind him. Mike closed the trunk and moved back to where the woman stood next to the open driver's side door. He had to get her moving before another vehicle arrived. "Go on and get behind the wheel." Mike urged her into the car. "Tell the police what happened."

"But I'm just a stripper."

Mike held her gaze. "You're a person with rights like everyone else. You've escaped a kidnapping thanks to a Good Samaritan."

"Okay." She swiped her tear-stained cheeks.

Mike patted his pockets, but he hadn't brought any real identification along tonight. "Ask for Officer Cooper at the Wilshire Precinct if you need more help."

"Okay."

"Hurry." Mike stepped back as she sped away.

He loped back to the Lotus, pleased to find Lauren waiting, though she was clearly antsy about the delay. "Mission accomplished."

"Thank God. I was worried sick." She straightened his tie and inhaled a big breath. "You're here now and one less woman is in danger."

It made him happier than he wanted to admit that she'd worried about him. *Keep your mind on the task, Stone.* Giving himself a mental kick, he drove up to the mansion and they joined the party without a glitch.

He'd suspected as much from the street, but walking in, he saw the place redefined ostentatious. Polzin had sunk a small fortune into this event and Mike wanted to destroy it all, thinking of the women who'd suffered so many indignities for the syndicate. The acres of marble, the gaudy flowers, and the apathetic waiters with silver trays serving drinks and hors d'oeuvres made Mike crave a pub with a long neck beer and a dartboard. He hid his contempt under a hard expression and an iron will, following Lauren's lead as his sexy as hell raven-haired assistant.

Crime happened everywhere. Mike was all too aware. But this? It was over the top offensive. Money and ego cloaked the room like a thick fog and the temptation to blow his cover, to attempt taking all of them down right now nearly overwhelmed him.

At his side, Lauren brushed her arm against his and he followed her glance toward a lavish set of doors at the far side of the main room. Vanya appeared first, leading the women from the school, each of them in a different jewel-toned gown. Did they have any idea why they were really here?

LAUREN SENSED the shifting focus in the room as the cocktail hour wound down and the wait staff drifted away. The women had been pleasant, smiling and chatting with each guest, though none of them approached Polzin and Vanya. This was the moment, their only window of opportunity. Polzin rose from a hideous white leather couch and buttoned his suit coat. The other men followed his lead, the movements rippling through the gathering like a pebble dropped into a quiet pond. Time for business.

Feeling Mike's gaze on her, she sent him what she

hoped qualified as an obedient expression as he filed out with the men. From the moment of their arrival, she'd mirrored his movements, examining the captive women as she might assess a cut of beef, despite her churning stomach. They were no more than cattle to these men. Beautiful, certainly more expensive, but definitely cattle. It was a wonder they weren't forced to parade about completely nude.

What could've brought Desmond into this horrible circle? Riding another burst of outrage, she didn't have to fake her harsh expression as she joined the other assistants herding the women into a luxurious, completely feminine salon. Plush seating areas in rose-toned upholstery had been accented with trays of champagne flutes brimming with extravagance. Under the guise of more closely examining each of the women on display, Lauren verified the placement of the two security cameras, the two doors, and the one guard. She caught Vanya's eye, hoping the tight smile on the Russian beauty's face was a positive sign.

"You!" Lauren snapped her fingers at a woman reaching for a flute of champagne. Everyone in the room turned her way. "Come here."

The young woman wore a sapphire silk gown, the plunging neckline drenched with strands of pearls that rattled softly as she walked. She'd likely been presented this way to appeal to one of Polzin's most valued customers. Lauren reached out and firmly wiped away the makeup covering the girl's black eye. "She is disobedient?" Lauren demanded of Vanya.

"Nonsense." Vanya rushed over. As Polzin's mistress it was her job to maintain calm and control during the waiting period in the salon. "This is an accident. She is a good girl."

Lauren huffed impatiently, taking her phone from her clutch and snapping a picture of the girl's injury. "We won't take this one or any other defective merchandise like her."

The security guard came at her and Vanya shooed the showcased women toward the far side of the room. Pretending devotion to Desmond had been small potatoes compared to tonight's performance. Lauren had to give Vanya the opportunity to get the women out. Her pulse pounded in her ears, but she held her ground as a wall of a man demanded her phone and told her to leave the room. Every step closer to her gave the women one more step closer to freedom.

"No," she replied. The only option was to plow through this nightmare. "I'm sure they are all equally unacceptable in some way." She hit send before he seized the device. "Polzin is slipping," she said, baiting the guard. "We all see it," she waved a hand, encompassing the other assistants trying to become invisible.

The guard kept his eyes on her. "You do not like the party? You can leave," he announced.

"I don't answer to you," she said. She raised her chin and crossed her arms. Over his shoulder she caught swift flashes of color as Vanya urged the women out of the room.

The guard gripped Lauren's elbow and hauled her toward the door she'd entered only minutes before. Lauren tried to dig her heels into the thick carpeting. She batted at him with her purse, making a ridiculous scene that kept all eyes on her.

When he reached for his communications link, she let loose the shrill, ear-splitting scream that horror movie directors adored. She stomped her sharp heel into the top of his foot, another move learned on the job, and practically leaped across the threshold into the hallway. She slammed the door as the others launched into a protest. Her hands shook as she turned the key Vanya had dropped into her clutch when she'd snapped that pic. The locked door wouldn't hold long but she only needed one more minute.

Racing down the main hallway toward the courtyard at the side of the house, she prayed Mike had escaped from his meeting. Her heels clattered against the marble floors, but she didn't slow down to mute the noise. If Vanya had second thoughts or changed her mind, their escape would turn ugly any second now. Vanya was supposed to crash through the main gate if necessary. Lauren prayed the getaway would work.

Raised voices echoed behind her. Lauren kept moving, bursting through a set of French doors and into the cool night air of the rear courtyard. She turned at the sound of an engine just as the last woman disappeared into a black SUV.

Behind the wheel of the SUV, Vanya threw the car into reverse and floored it, heedless of the ruined paint jobs and dents of other vehicles she left in her wake.

"They're clear."

Lauren whipped around. Mike. Thank God!

"We have to move." Mike grabbed her hand. "This way."

"Does she know where she's going?" Lauren hesitated, watching the SUV disappear. She couldn't help worrying that Vanya would simply circle back and return the women to the mansion.

"I programmed the navigation system and sent an alert to an old friend in the Highway Patrol and another friend who's in town. Claudia is on standby if something goes wrong." Mike held out his hand. "We can talk on the way. Let's go."

His skin was warm, his grip strong as he linked his fingers with hers. They scooted toward the line of elite vehicles, shouts dogging their steps. Bullets abruptly chipped away at the rock framing the central fountain as they hurried past. Lauren kept pace, trusting Mike to hold up his end of their risky plan.

They were nearly to the end of the driveway when he yanked the car door open and pushed her into the passenger side of their Lotus. The tight hem of her dress ripped as she struggled to right herself. Lauren clicked her seatbelt into place as Mike roared down the hill and away from the house. The gate was open, one side lying on the ground. The guard took a shot at them, hitting a fender but missing the tire as they whizzed past him.

"We can't get too far ahead of them," she reminded him. "Did you catch anything useful in there?"

"You mean besides the identities of the seller and all those local buyers of abducted women and the terms negotiated?" His attention darted between the road in front of them and the pursuers closing in. "I'm certain I gave a performance they'll all regret for the next twenty years to life."

"Then we did it!" Lauren laughed. "We did it!"

A bullet pinged off the driver's side mirror. Lauren screamed.

"Hang on," Mike ordered as he rammed the accelerator.

The Lotus rocketed forward and stole her breath.

MIKE KEPT his eyes locked on the street and the lights

of Los Angeles spreading out before them. He didn't dare look at Lauren or he'd drive right off the road at this speed. His body might be accustomed to the rush of adrenaline, but something was different about tonight from any of his previous missions for either the military or private sector.

The answer—damned obvious—was sitting in the passenger seat. He couldn't ignore the facts. He'd fallen for her. Against all sense and better judgment, he'd fallen hard for her. He might tell her. If they lived through the next few hours, he'd have earned the right to tell her.

"Take off the wig," he ordered. "Get as Lauren Marie Woods as you can."

"What are you thinking? I'm still a person of interest in a murder investigation."

"Exactly," he answered. "Let's create a Lauren Marie sighting to bring out a police response."

"You can't possibly believe a cop or two will deter Polzin's henchmen?"

"We just need the bastard to blink," he said, pleased when she tossed the black wig to the floor and removed the contacts. "I'll give the car to a valet and we'll hit a packed club. We can get away on foot."

"On foot? Oh my God. You're serious."

"I still have a friend or two in this town."

She slapped a hand against the door as the sleek car leaned into a curve. "Will you introduce me?"

He smiled, changing lanes to get around a dawdling truck. "They'll ask you for autographs."

"No way. You have friends who watch Harper Cove?"

He laughed, willing the car to reach the city before Polzin's men caught them. "No, honey. I have friends who'd be happy to make some easy cash selling a Lauren Marie Woods autograph."

"Oh. That makes more sense."

If he'd expected a rant, he would've been disappointed. Another actress might've gone off on him for that crack, but not Lauren. She kept him on his toes and he liked it. "You took that news easily enough."

"Blame it on priorities." She looked back. "The mobsters are gaining on us."

He glanced in the rearview mirror, knowing this would be too close for comfort, if they made it at all. Two big SUVs were closing in on them. "Lauren, if this backfires—"

"Where's your gun?" she asked, interrupting him.

"Seized at the mansion."

"Damn it."

He agreed. A few more blocks and Polzin's men would have to shoot or come after them on foot. The phone in her purse started ringing. Only Claudia—and Polzin—had the number. As Lauren answered, he prayed it was good news while he navigated the increasing traffic on his way to The Vibe, an LA club owned by Derrick, one of his best friends from high school. He didn't want to bring hell raining down on the place, but he might not have a choice.

"Well?" he asked when she dropped the phone back into her purse.

"Claudia says Vanya and the other women made it to the FBI office. Claudia had two agents standing by."

"Good." He felt her watching him and wondered what she was thinking.

"You've been holding out on me."

He wasn't surprised by the assessment. Lauren was a quick study. Not just with a costume and a role, but with everything life threw at her. She kept pushing on regardless of the obstacles, determined to reach her goals. Right now it was simple survival, but after that... well he knew she wanted to do big things on and off camera. And he wanted to be there.

He was done suppressing his attraction to her and her multi-faceted life. She was a once in a lifetime kind of woman and he didn't want to walk away when the case was over. Somewhere along the way, Lauren had become more than a client. He had to find a way to let her know, to show her he was sincere. Then, if the attraction and personal interest only went one-way he'd deal with the consequences.

She had no idea what he'd been withholding and

chalking up to Claudia's assistance. When he'd first met her, he saw her only as another client who didn't need to know his friends or connections in California. Hell, he'd been ignoring his friends and connections since he'd returned from the Navy.

But all that had flipped on him while working this case for her. He was about to bring her into The Vibe as herself. That hadn't exactly been what Derrick had agreed to. His friend would either give him a high five for sending influential faces this way tonight or punch him for bringing the Krushka syndicate so close. As Mike veered into the valet lane, he braced for anything.

Well, anything but Lauren. The rip in her dress only served to display more of those gorgeous legs when she emerged from the Lotus. With a toss of her long blond hair and a sparkling laugh, she had him believing the murder accusation the fantasy here. She amazed him.

The big SUVs behind them rolled right on by with the flow of traffic. The windows were lowered, but no one opened fire. Had the change in disguise thrown them off or had they been called so resolve the problem differently? Worry niggled at him. Whatever the case, Mike knew better than to assume that meant the chase was over. He reached for Lauren, enjoying the way her hand curled around his bicep as she leaned into him. He might not be armed, but for her, he could conquer any trouble with his bare hands.

At the door, they were ushered inside and merging with the crowd on the dance floor within moments. Personal connections were a good thing, Mike realized for the first time in a long time. Derrick had promised his staff would grant Mike and Lauren full access tonight. It was a calculated risk, knowing Polzin's men might attack the club, but they would've been cornered at the hotel or the safe house and he couldn't take that chance.

"Your friend owns The Vibe?"

He nodded.

"Mike." She pressed her body close to his as though her hips were compelled by the music. "You're full of intriguing secrets."

More than she knew. He brushed his mouth across hers, his palms sliding over the thin fabric wrapped around her hips. He wanted her out of the clothes, away from everything related to this case. He wanted her. With him. No secrets, no roles, no looming threats. "You gave a stunning performance tonight," he murmured against her lips.

"So you do like me with dark hair."

"I don't." He shook his head, forced himself to scan the dance floor. "I need a drink." Anything strong enough to dull his desire was out of the question, because it would give the Russians an edge. He ordered a beer and she asked for the same. With the longneck bottles in hand, they made slow progress to the opposite side of the dance floor.

Derrick had given him the code for the suite upstairs and he wanted to retreat to that quiet safety. First they had to make sure plenty of people saw her here, living it up. She was bait again, but this time for the police.

They danced, using the crowd as a shield to move through the club while Russians skulked near the exits in standard predator procedure. Too bad the prey wasn't leaving.

"Can you give me a hint?" she asked, her gaze sliding toward the men from Polzin's operation. "A time frame?"

He bent his head to her ear. "We'll move when the police arrive. I've got this."

She graced him with a wide, genuine smile. "I trust you."

His blood turned hot in his veins. He recognized the sweet stab of lust when she peered up at him through her long eyelashes, but he wanted something else from her. Something he wasn't sure she wanted to give to him or any other man.

It took longer than he'd hoped for the distraction and commotion as police arrived flashing badges but not guns. "Now we move." He drifted into the shadows with her and through a staff-only access door.

"This way," he said, nudging her into a stairwell.

"Up one more flight. Derrick has a private suite stocked and outfitted with monitors." And much more. "He's letting us hide here tonight."

"Won't the police search the place for me?"

"Claudia is already working on drawing them away with another Lauren Marie sighting."

"But Polzin's men won't give up on us," she said pausing at the landing. "Not after we helped Vanya and the women escape."

"They won't get to us here."

"You're sure?"

"I promise." He brushed his knuckles across her perfect cheek.

She studied him a long moment, then nodded. "Lead the way," she said, lacing her fingers with his once more.

He hoped she meant that as he entered the code and drew her into the suite. He couldn't remember ever wanting a woman the way he wanted her. She stirred a dark need inside him. He wanted to worship every sensual curve of her body, master the things that brought her pleasure, and unveil every nuance of the woman behind the persona. He'd never experienced the pounding demand he felt with her. More troubling, he felt sure he would never experience it with anyone else.

He stopped inside the door and pushed his hands through her hair. Tugging gently, her chin came up, exposing the pale column of her throat. Pressing his lips to that soft, warm flesh, he felt the quickening of her pulse. "I need you." It was an understatement, but he wasn't in any condition to deliver a monologue.

She pushed her hands under his suit jacket, her fingers tugging at his shirt. "It's mutual. Do we dare? There are cops and bad guys just downstairs—all looking for us."

"Oh we dare, baby."

He kissed her, hard, giving her a hint of what he sought. She opened for him, drew his tongue into her mouth, and arched her body against him.

He broke the kiss long enough to catch his breath and flip on a light. "Fully stocked," he said. "Derrick said to help ourselves."

She licked her lips, her gaze locked on his mouth. "You're my only craving."

Thank God for common ground. "Same goes." His hands clutching her rounded hips, his mouth fused with hers as he backed her into the room until she bumped into the back of the sectional. Nothing would stop them this time. It took every ounce of strength to slow down. He was all too ready for her, too eager to act on the fantasies he'd built around her. If he only had tonight, he'd make it count. "Turn around."

Her eyelids fluttered open and her pale eyes smoldered with heat. He waited, wondering if his struggle for self-control showed on his face. Finally she turned, giving him her back. "Lift your hair." He smiled as she gathered the long tresses into her hands, revealing a wealth of creamy, silky skin. "Hold still."

She complied and he pressed his lips to her nape as he slowly lowered the zipper on her dress. He tasted every fresh inch of skin on the way down and back up again, relishing every little tremor and moan.

"So responsive," he murmured as his palms cruised over her body. He reached around and weighed her breasts in his hands. She arched into his touch as he brought her nipples to hard peaks. Flexing his hips he rocked his erection against her ass, leaving no doubt what her reactions were doing to him.

"I want to touch you," she said.

"In time." He caught her wrists and lowered her arms, until her hands rested in the hollow just above her hips. Keeping out of her reach, he turned her and claimed her mouth again.

Sliding the thin straps of her dress over her shoulders, he stripped away the fabric, exploring her with his hands and mouth until only her heels and lacy panties remained.

He traced the scalloped edge of lace with his tongue, teasing a nervous laugh out of her. He wanted her at his mercy, no disguises, no role-play. Tonight he wanted all of her, the real woman, the brave woman behind the successful entertainer. He wanted more than that, but he didn't have the words.

With his hands and mouth, he explored every rise and hollow of her body. Drawing away that last bit of lace, he teased her with his tongue and fingers, giving her everything he couldn't articulate. He licked and teased, letting the sensations build and learning what made her pant and sigh. Breathing in her arousal, sliding his fingers deep into her wet channel, he pushed her until her knees quaked. When she surrendered completely on a shuddering climax, his relished the way she called his name, her hands holding him close.

His body caressed hers as he stood and she trembled with the aftershocks. He caught her in his arms and settled her across his lap on the sectional. The heat of her scorched him through his trousers, made his body ache to thrust. She pressed soft kisses to his neck, his ear before she tugged his chin around so she could claim his mouth. He nearly pounced on her, all too eager to drive himself into her hot, wet body.

"You're overdressed," she whispered, nipping his jaw with her teeth as her fingertips worked at his shirtfront.

"Do you want to fix that?"

"Oh, yes." She sat up, her nude body surrounding him in open invitation as her legs straddled his. "Can I have my way with you?"

"Always." The answer was out there and he didn't even want to snatch it back. He knew, beyond any doubt, he'd always be hers. But this wasn't the time to discuss it.

"*Mmm.*" Her eyes sparkled with mischief. "I'm a lucky woman."

He wasn't about to argue as she dispensed with his jacket and shirt, her hands running over his skin and setting him on fire. She stood and pulled him to his feet. When she dropped to her knees in front of him, he lost his breath. He lifted one foot at a time for her to remove his shoes and socks. Her delicate fingers unfastened his belt and trousers and slowly worked them down his legs. He stepped out of them, his body shuddering as she touched him through the silk boxer briefs. He closed his eyes and prayed he would survive as she slowly tugged away that last barrier. She pressed her lips to his hip, her cheek brushing his erection. She gave him one exquisite lick from base to tip.

No more. He pulled her up, but she wasn't ready to relinquish control. She pushed him back onto the sofa. With her hands braced on his shoulders, she lowered her hips over his erection in one smooth motion. Slick with passion, her body clutched and released his length as she glided up and down. He filled his hands and mouth with her breasts as her head fell back and her eyes closed on a little moan of pleasure.

His desire spiked as he watched her react to his touch, inside and out. His body jerked and he gripped her hips, holding her tight against him as the climax crashed over them both like a wave.

Here's the real Lauren, he thought as she collapsed against him with a satisfied sigh. He didn't deserve her, he knew it, but he intended to do everything in his power to keep her in his life.

CHAPTER 12

LAUREN WASN'T sure where her body stopped and Mike's began. His heartbeat, pounding under her hand, felt more real than her own. She needed to move, but couldn't quite make it happen.

He'd thoroughly exposed her, body and soul, and she wanted to start all over again. She pressed her lips to the hot skin of his shoulder and tried to catch her breath. Pleasure seemed like too tame a word for what they'd shared. For the woman who kept herself under control in all things, surrendering to him left her feeling cherished and precious rather than just a useful toy or convenience.

He'd asked for the real Lauren and she'd given him all of her, allowing him to see a side of her she didn't realize she'd had. She eased back, the air chilling her skin as their bodies parted, but he stilled her with his hand splayed across her lower back.

"Not without a kiss," he said.

Lauren happily obliged, letting her mind fade to a blank canvas as she sank into the tastes and sensations that were uniquely him. Reluctantly shifting away from him, she slipped into his dress shirt as she stood up. Catching the possessive look in his eyes, she smiled to herself as she wandered off to find the bathroom. That look should've scared her. It didn't.

She'd seen possessiveness lead people down dark trails of obsession and worse. But when Mike gave her that look, she felt secure in a way she'd never experienced or expected. She'd suspected from that first day that letting him close could be addictive. Tonight's events from the rescue to the escape to the magnificent sex proved her theory beyond all doubt. It was strange to realize she wouldn't regret a single minute of her time with him.

They'd taken risks and they'd been in serious danger, but survived. Together. She'd been more than a little scared for Vanya and those women and herself, but she realized her confidence in Mike had never wavered.

When she emerged from the bathroom, he'd straightened up and pulled on his slacks, and was staring intently at his phone. "What now?" she asked, savoring the view of his muscled torso. She'd had her hands all over that sculpted body. A delicious tremor slid through her. She hoped he would be game for an encore.

"Now." Standing, he walked over and took her hand, raising it to his lips. "We rest. Tomorrow we'll take what we have to the feds." He led her toward the bed. "Derrick says this place is ours for as long as we need it."

His connections from Sadie's husband to the owner of this club surprised her, as he kept so much of himself locked away. Private. At first, she'd assumed it was merely professional distance, but now she could see him clearly. He was afraid his friends, like his father, believed the worst of him. She knew how that felt, understood what it was like when the public persona didn't match the truth, but couldn't be corrected without making things worse. "You have a good friend."

"Yeah." He pulled back the bedding. "Ladies first."

He expected her to sleep? That felt far more intimate than sex, but she slid between the cool sheets, happy just to be near him. "What aren't you telling me?"

The mattress dipped a little as he stretched out beside her. "It can wait."

She studied the shadows in his eyes, the tension in his jaw. Whatever he'd learned, he knew she wouldn't like it. "I'd rather hear it now."

"Vanya is dead."

"What?" Lauren sat up. The euphoria of success evaporated in an instant as shock and anger rolled through her. Tears welled in her eyes, blurring her vision. "That's impossible. We got them out. They went to the authorities."

Mike sat up and gathered her into his arms. "Polzin guessed right. He knew her better than we thought he did. Claudia learned that Vanya gave her statement, but was killed in transit to an FBI safe house."

Lauren curled into Mike's strength. A statement wouldn't be as effective as a witness in a courtroom. "This has to stop." She dried her tears with the edge of the sheet. "We have to find a way to stop him."

"The others are safe. That will be enough to put him behind bars."

Lauren disagreed. "His men will take the fall for the kidnappings and the crimes at the school. You know as well as I do that tonight won't put a dent in his operation. He'll just keep supplying those awful buyers."

"I have names and faces on video, Lauren. We'll turn over everything tomorrow morning."

"This has gone too far," she insisted.

"*Shh.*" He pulled her close. "Rest now." His hand stroked through her hair, soothing her. "I promise Polzin will pay."

"But Vanya…" Lauren's voice trailed off on a wave of grief. While Vanya wasn't a friend, there'd been some camaraderie. They had shared a mutual goal and determination to break the horrid organization Desmond had helped Polzin create here.

When they'd first identified Polzin, Mike had warned her about the dangers and the cost of failure. She'd believed him, and yet she'd also believed he was close enough to invincible that it would all work out perfectly. She'd been more than willing to step up and stop this madness, but she'd never allowed herself to envision anyone getting hurt. Or dead.

She shook her head. "I can't sleep. Not now."

"Just close your eyes. Let it all go. For an hour." His hand worked some magic on her skin, in her hair, lulling her into a twilight doze where the sting of failure wasn't quite as sharp. "Just an hour," he murmured.

MIKE KEPT SOOTHING her until her breath evened out and her body relaxed. She'd been through an ordeal, followed by one shock after another as they'd peeled back the layers Trinity had used to insulate himself from Polzin and the law.

While Lauren slept, Mike reviewed every detail, looking for his mistake. Saving the redhead from the party had potentially put Polzin on alert and while they'd escaped, he knew Polzin wasn't done. Not with Lauren and not with his lucrative human trafficking operation. The feds had a good start with Vanya's statement supporting the claims of those women, Trinity and Polzin's ownership of the finishing school and the club. But Lauren was right. Polzin could still slip free.

She snuggled closer to him and his body responded, but not with lust or passion. No, like a reflex he automatically curled around her, giving her shelter despite their safe surroundings. What was wrong with him? He told himself to get up, to go sleep on the couch until they needed to leave, but he couldn't do it. Hadn't his dad always said he invested too quickly in people?

It had been true enough with Lauren.

Thinking of his old man typically irritated him. Not this time. Quick or not, investing in Lauren as a client and a woman felt right. There was no use fighting it, so he let the feeling wash over him. He didn't have to know right here and now what they would do about their connection, about this need for her building inside him. Those answers could wait until the biggest dangers in her life were once more paparazzi, happy fans, and competition for choice roles.

SATURDAY, *December 13*

MIKE MANAGED a couple hours of sleep, rising as the sun shimmered on the edge of the eastern horizon.

He didn't need a window or a clock, his body knew when to get moving.

Sliding away from Lauren's tempting body, he showered and borrowed a shirt from his friend since Lauren still wore his. It wouldn't take any time for a club limo to get them to the safe house where they could change into something less provocative for the interview with the feds.

He returned to the bedroom to wake her up, but she was sitting on the edge of the bed waiting for him. "Good morning."

She shrugged. "Any coffee?"

"In a bar?" He grinned. "Always."

"Good." She pushed her hands through her hair. "I've been thinking about Polzin and Desmond."

He would've been surprised if she hadn't. "And?"

"We've followed everything but the money."

"You said all his money was tied up in the agency and his other companies."

"I'm wrong. I must be if Claudia couldn't find it," she said, gathering her hair into a loose ponytail. "I woke up thinking about Vanya, about why she was at the office with Desmond that night."

Mike waited, but she didn't elaborate. "Hold that thought." He went out to the kitchen and started a pot of coffee for her, then grabbed a cola from the refrigerator for himself.

Lauren joined him, wearing the dress from last

night. "Even you said she agreed too quickly to help us." Lauren watched the fresh coffee fill the carafe.

"But she didn't betray us," he replied. "She got the women out. She saved them."

"And paid the ultimate price." Lauren dropped her head into her hands, but when she looked up again her eyes were clear. "Desmond did terrible things, but what if he and Vanya were together because they wanted to escape Polzin?"

"In your police statement you said Trinity claimed he'd stopped sending product because of legal scrutiny."

She sighed. "Desmond always said whatever suited his purposes in the moment. Implying a federal investigation sounds much better than admitting you're trying to help the boss's mistress escape. We can confirm my theory easy enough when we meet with the FBI."

"True." He'd been with the buyers long enough for a firsthand look at Polzin's ruthless streak. The women they'd rescued were samples, meant to be tokens to ease the impatience for the real shipment. Polzin had ordered Vanya's death, but he'd be looking for Mike and Lauren now. Mike knew that, and while he trusted Lauren's disguises and Claudia's skills at erasing a trail, they wouldn't be safe until Polzin was behind bars or dead.

They'd embarrassed a powerful, narcissistic man. The mob boss would have to retaliate and quickly or someone would try to take over his operation. "How would Trinity and Vanya have expected to get away with their plan and how can we turn that back on Polzin?"

"After getting caught in Desmond's office, Vanya was dead whether she helped us or not," Lauren suggested. "She must have sensed that Polzin was growing unhappy with her. It's the only thing that explains her willingness to help us. She likely knew it was just a matter of time before he figured out what she'd really been up to. Not to mention, she was getting older. She surely understood that would become an issue soon."

Mike couldn't argue with her logic. "How do we prove it? How do we use it?"

"There's a safe in Desmond's house. I wouldn't have considered it before, but knowing what we know now it's worth a look." She shrugged. "We have nothing to lose but time."

"Chances are Polzin's men have already been there."

Lauren shook her head. "They'd never find it. I lived there and I found it by accident after four years of never knowing it was there."

"But can you open it?"

She smiled. "Desmond used the same password for everything. His code for his security system at home and the office was the same. I'll bet the combination for the safe is the same or close enough for me to guess."

"For a clever guy, he wasn't so smart. What's the password?"

Lauren grabbed her clutch purse. "The letters g-o-d plus Desmond's birthday."

"The guy had an ego, that's for sure." Mike put his jacket around her shoulders. "Let's see what we can find."

"I really need to change."

"We can stop by the safe house for clothes."

When she put her hand in his, he felt like he could conquer the world. For her. Navy SEAL training had honed his body and his skills, giving him confidence to tackle any situation until he'd had no choice but to become the scapegoat on the op that ended his career. He'd let that fiasco get into his head. Sure his dad had refused to speak with him since the incident. The old man had always been tough. Becoming a SEAL had been Mike's only worthy accomplishment in his dad's eyes. His departure from that career had ruined the one thing about him his dad respected. While Mike had long ago given up on a relationship with his father, he'd never noticed that he kept the rest of the world at arm's length after that, too. Until this case required a little extra help from an unexpected source, he'd avoided his old friends, using his surfboard and the ocean for companionship. He'd never thought of it as a problem before.

Lauren changed all that. Not just her case. Her. She turned him inside out, made him assess and reevaluate. He wasn't sure he liked it, but he was damned sure he didn't want to go on without it.

9:15 a.m.

FROM THE BACK of the limo Derrick provided, Mike watched to ensure they weren't followed as he sent instructions to Claudia. Lauren stared at the cityscape passing by the windows. "You'll need a new disguise for today," he said, pocketing his phone. He was almost looking forward to what she might come up with this time. "Polzin will be scouring the city looking for us."

She gave him a weary smile. "Renae Ford was a one-night wonder. I think today is a job for Lauren Marie Woods and Mike Stone."

"If you're sure."

She nodded and put her hand in his. Again, he found himself wanting to say something profound and meaningful, something to boost her morale, but any words that came to mind turned to dust on his tongue.

At the safe house, she showered and they changed clothes in separate bedrooms, meeting in the kitchen to review the best approach to Trinity's house. Being in the same room with her as she changed would have him struggling for control again.

"Do you want a gun?" he asked.

"No thanks," she replied. "Can I call Officer Cooper?"

"Not a bad idea." He handed her his phone, listening as she left a quick message with Trinity's address and her intention to pick up a few things. "That should get some attention."

"Let's hope it's the right kind of attention."

She was quiet for the duration of the drive to Trinity's neighborhood. He was tempted to draw her out, worried she wasn't ready for what they'd find, but he didn't want to make things worse. He cruised by the house and, not spotting anyone from either side of the law watching it, he parked the Camaro a block away. The media circus was long gone. The buzz shifted quickly in Hollywood.

They walked the short distance in silence and her code opened the back gate on the first try. It felt too easy but who, aside from the alarm company, had the need or ability to change the code?

"Where's the safe?" he asked when they were inside.

She pointed to a doorway tucked under the stairwell behind the kitchen. "This way." She led him past the rows of well-organized shelves and revealed a pull away unit. She entered the code and the safe door swung open. He saw stacks of jewelry boxes on one side, cash on the other. No movie-worthy ledger, no passports or travel documents. Not even a notebook of his transactions with Polzin or the finishing school.

"His passport is missing," she said. "Desmond must have had that with him. No one else would have known to look here."

She was right on both counts, but that small relief didn't squelch his prickling instincts. Maybe it was just the close confines of the glorified closet, but he felt trapped. "We need to go."

"This may be our best and final chance to connect Desmond to Polzin. We should keep looking."

"We'll find another way." The small window near the ceiling wouldn't give them a decent escape if they were caught in here. It boiled down to keeping her safe and with every passing second he sensed more danger in this situation.

"Wait." Lauren started pulling the jewelry out of the safe and stacking it on the floor. "There has to be something we can use. At least a clue."

Mike sympathized. As much as he hated obeying a retreat order, sometimes it was the best option. The federal investigators could sort out this mess. So what if he had to hide her a bit longer? Neither of them had family to miss them. They'd find a secluded spot near the coast. Maybe Hawaii. He'd surf, she'd disguise herself when they wanted to go out. The mysterious disappearance of Lauren Marie Woods would only strengthen her comeback a few months or even years from now. He'd figure out a way to make it sound logical later. First, they had to get out of here.

"Got it," she said, her voice breathless as she stared into a long, slim jewelry box. "It's so sick. And simple." She unfolded several sheets of paper stashed in another velvet box. "If I'm reading this right, they placed orders for women with gemstones. Diamonds for blondes, sapphires for brunettes, and rubies for redheads. That's why the women were dressed in those sequined gowns last night." She shook her head. "This page is just the past year. It shows deposits into an account I don't recognize." She handed that box to him and reached for another. "Oh my God. It's the same. This has to be some sort of crazy accounting system."

Mike put the box back on the stack. He wanted to hear all about it, preferably with a trustworthy FBI agent recording it all. "Let's lock it up. We'll tell the feds all about it, but right now we have to go."

With a nod, she put everything back in place and locked the safe. As she exited the closet, she skidded to a stop. Mike looked past her to the two men waiting just inside the backdoor. Peter Kozlov and his muscle Nikoli Maksimov.

"Good morning, Miss Woods," Kozlov said. "Mr. Polzin will be delighted to see you."

Mike stepped between Lauren and the threat. He wasn't about to let them take her without a fight. "Polzin will have to be disappointed, Kozlov."

Both men glared at him. "You are of no consequence to Mr. Polzin."

"I know your names and your rap sheets," Mike explained. "In fact, you're starring in a documentary I made just last night. You might remember it? There were women being sold."

Maksimov reached for his gun.

"That's not necessary," Lauren began, but Mike leaped into action.

He jumped straight for the weapon like a soldier throwing himself over a grenade. Startled by the unexpected move, Maksimov stumbled back and Mike let the momentum carry them into Kozlov. "Run!" he shouted to Lauren as the gun skittered across floor. He pounded the enforcer's head against the unyielding tile, hoping it would keep him down while he dealt with Kozlov.

A gunshot froze him mid-attack and he feared the worst as he obeyed Kozlov's order to stand. The kitchen was suddenly full of glowering, oversized Russians. He and Lauren were outnumbered. In their eagerness to pile on the charges against Polzin, they'd walked right into a trap. Another enforcer had Lauren's hair in a harsh grip and her elbows pinned behind her. At the all-clear signal, Polzin walked in as if he owned the place. Mike nearly laughed. Hell, after everything they'd learned about Trinity that might be true. Mike's jaw clenched as Polzin's gaze raked Lauren from head to toe. No way he'd let that bastard touch her.

"At last the lovely Lauren Marie Woods shall be my mistress," Polzin announced in a conversational tone.

What the hell? Mike started forward but Maksimov's weapon bored deeper into his skull.

"Never." Lauren shook her head despite the grip of the thug holding her.

"You will," Polzin gripped her chin, leaning close. "It is only fitting that Desmond's woman will replace the woman he turned against me."

She spat in his face.

Mike's heart almost stalled even as he found her bravery magnificent. The woman wouldn't back down from anything. This wasn't an act, it was simply one facet of what made her so special.

Polzin struck her hard across the cheek.

Mike saw red, fury exploding inside him. Polzin would suffer for touching her. To hell with evidence and feds. To hell with professionalism. The bastard had just sealed his fate.

"You will learn to please me." A sly smile tilted his lips. "Or you will die trying."

Mike made up his mind right then and there. Whether Lauren realized it yet or not, she belonged with him. When this was over, Polzin dead and the others in custody, they would have a serious discussion.

Studying the men surrounding them, Mike knew it would be an uphill battle, but he would win. Mentally, he prepared himself to seize the first opportunity to regain control of the situation.

Polzin was going down.

CHAPTER 13

LAUREN WATCHED, horrified, as Maksimov and two other burly enforcers took turns pummeling Mike. Two would hold him up while the third drove fists and knees into his torso. He gasped and doubled over as they drove the air from his lungs and punished his kidneys. Tears welled in her eyes as they dragged him out of the kitchen and tossed him into the trunk of the limousine Polzin had arrived in.

Though he didn't hit her again, Polzin stared her down and, with excruciating calm, made her two options crystal clear. She could get in the limo with him or die right here in Desmond's kitchen. She followed him outside and hurried to obey when his driver opened the door. Sliding across the leather seat she struggled to mentally prepare for a life-saving performance.

Whatever it took to protect Mike.

Polzin and his men obviously didn't consider her a physical threat. He'd waved off the suggestion of tying her up and he'd chosen to sit next to her in the passenger compartment with no bodyguard.

She could feel time running out, rushing away from her. When the driver took Santa Monica Boulevard, she assumed they were heading for the finishing school. If Polzin managed to reach the school, she knew he'd never let them leave alive. Making the mental adjustment, she considered her limited options, struggling to remember if Vanya had telegraphed any of Polzin's weaknesses. She thought back to those brief minutes in the dressing room, replaying Vanya's interaction with him.

All men had a chink in their armor. It was a matter of finding it and applying the right pressure. Polzin was over-confident, but she couldn't possibly overpower him. "What must I do?" she asked, pitching her voice into a desperate whisper.

"Everything I require." He leaned forward. "Peter wanted you. If you displease me, I will let him have you. His preferences run darker than mine, if you can imagine it."

She didn't want to imagine anything about either of them. She crossed her legs at the ankle and kept her gaze lowered. "What will it take to save my friend's life?"

"Forget him. He is likely dying already of internal injuries." Polzin's mouth twisted into a malevolent grimace. "A collapsed lung, perhaps. My men know how to cause suffering."

"He was only trying to protect me. Please let him go."

"No."

"I'll do anything you ask." She raised her gaze, risking eye contact with her captor. "He's important to me."

"He will be *nothing* to you," Polzin barked. He leaned close, his moist breath hot on her cheek. "My wishes are important to you now. *I* am your world, Lauren. You will breathe, eat, and dress on my command and no other."

She looked away. "I-I understand."

His hard fingers dug hard into her chin, forcing her to face him. "Not yet, but you will. In time."

Lauren knew Polzin expected absolute obedience. She needed to show him the terrified woman, the defeated girl too weak to challenge him. This, she realized, was the most important performance of her life. She had to play it perfectly. Her heart stuttered as the driver took a sharp turn and she was pressed into Polzin. No one followed them except the big black car Kozlov drove.

Had Officer Cooper ignored her message? Had it been intercepted? She battled against the fear of failure, knowing she had less than an hour before they reached the school. If no help came, she would improvise. She would make a scene that would stall this convoy while there was still a chance for help to arrive.

Several more minutes passed in a charged silence as the limousine and the escort car flowed through traffic. Every minute that passed was another one Mike suffered from his injuries with no help. She had to do something soon.

"Did Desmond ever tell you that you were the catalyst for his finishing school?"

Polzin's words made her shudder. She shook her head. He clutched her chin in an iron grip once more and made her look at him.

"You will always answer me with words and the proper respect."

"Yes, sir." He released her and she leaned back into the seat cushions, withdrawing as far from him as she dared.

"That is better." Polzin stroked her thigh gently, making her feel more and more like a dog being trained by a hard master. "We knew each other from parties and such. The first moment I saw you, I wanted you, but he negotiated a more lucrative deal. He would provide me with whatever I desired and he would keep you."

Her stomach knotted. Desmond had been forced into this scheme in an effort to keep her away from Polzin all these years? Why hadn't he told her? She wasn't so sure that was all there was to it... she wasn't ready to see Desmond as any sort of hero.

"You were worth six flawless, blond women to him. Six!" His laughter dripped with cruelty. "Did you know you had such value?"

"No, sir," she replied quickly.

"That deal was a strong beginning for our business here. I had Desmond where I wanted him. We enjoyed much success."

She smothered the chill of dread sliding down her spine. Since he hadn't posed a question, she hoped her silence would be acceptable.

"I should have recognized you in Vanya's dressing room. Your disguise was brilliant. Seeing your body, even when I had no idea it was you, aroused me. Few women possess that power."

Bile rose in her throat. She swallowed it back.

"*Hmm.*" He studied her for a long time, his dark eyes cold and calculating. "Desmond had an eye for excellent quality and he kept you to himself. You will show me why he valued you so. Now."

"Here?" She had her answer as he loosened his belt, but a new hope shimmered when she spotted the grip of a handgun at his waist. If she could get the gun, she might give them a chance.

The car swayed as the driver accelerated along the curves of the PCH. Soon they would be at the school. She hoped Claudia and Mike's contacts would come through. Steeling herself, she covered Polzin's hands with hers. "Desmond valued my discretion," she murmured, peering at Polzin through her lashes.

On a grunt, Polzin raised the privacy screen. "Show me what else he valued. On your knees," he ordered, removing the obnoxious gun and placing it on the seat beside his thigh.

Pushing the humiliation to the back of her mind, she positioned herself between his legs, rocking a little as the car swerved with the road again. Her survival instincts surged into high gear. As seductively as she knew how, she slid his belt free of the buckle, catching her lower lip between her teeth. She had to sell it, had to make him believe she'd accepted she was at his mercy. Unfastening his slacks, she lifted his shirt out of the way, careful to keep her eyes off the gun.

A siren sounded nearby and Polzin grabbed her hands, his grip grinding the bones together painfully. "What did you do?"

"Nothing. Sir," she added quickly, looking around.

He yanked her back up to the seat and tore at her clothing. "Are you wired?" He shoved her jacket off her shoulders and stripped away her shirt.

"No!"

The siren closed in. "Where is your phone!"

"In my purse!" She resisted the urge to look for whatever vehicle was making the noise and prayed enough help had arrived to take him out.

He raised his hand to strike her, but the car swerved as the driver turned toward the canyon and his fist mercifully connected with leather instead of her face. "What have you done?" he screamed.

"I didn't do anything," she wailed, mounting fear for Mike bringing real tears now.

The limousine engine growled as the driver floored it, but he'd waited too long, the first incline was too steep. She could see the red and blue lights flashing through the windows now. There was no escape for Polzin on the two-lane road.

In a fury, Polzin lowered the privacy screen and shouted at his driver. The police were close, but the driver clearly had orders to keep going.

Lauren fumbled about the back seat for the gun, but it slid out of her reach. She searched frantically for another distraction. Finding the strap of her purse, she rolled it around her hand and swung it at Polzin's head. The blow only annoyed him and he lunged for her once more.

She scurried out of his reach. The back seat suddenly exploded inward. To Lauren's shock Mike finished kicking the seat out of his way and launched himself into the passenger compartment. "Get back!" he shouted, lunging for Polzin.

"There's a gun!" she warned, scrambling as far away from the fight as the car allowed. She prayed Mike would get his hands on the weapon first.

A loud report ripped through the air, followed quickly by a second gunshot. Polzin bellowed what were surely dire threats and curses in Russian. From the floorboards, she watched the blood ooze between Polzin's fingers as he grabbed for his thigh just above the knee. Based on the sudden swearing from the front seat, the second bullet must've hit the driver. The car jerked toward the dangerous edge of the road and Mike pitched himself across Polzin and the divider and into the front seat.

Lauren held her breath as Mike fought the driver. She prayed they weren't about to go careening down into the canyon. The car didn't tip or tumble, but it kept rolling forward. She rushed for the door on hands and knees, ready to get out the instant the car stopped. A brutal grip seized her ankle.

"Not so fast," Polzin said. "You are mine."

She kicked at his face as he tugged her closer, her hands clutching for anything she could use as a weapon. Her fingertips caught in her purse strap again and she brought it along as Polzin fought to subdue her.

She refused to go down easy, refused to let him off without a few scars to take with him. For Vanya, she thought, fighting to get the purse strap over his head. For every woman they were too late to save, she would fill Polzin with regrets. He dodged her attempts to gain an advantage. She would not give up. She fought harder, grabbing at the bastard's tie.

For Mike, she thought, who might be killed before she could tell him how much she loved every pushy, ripped, treasured inch of him.

"Pull over," Mike ordered, pressing the barrel of Polzin's gun against the driver's temple.

The driver swerved into the oncoming lane. Mike swore. It would be bad enough to fail, worse if that failure included death for him or Lauren, but the last thing this case needed was collateral damage. He reached out and yanked the wheel, keeping them closer to the correct lane. "Pull over or I'll shoot."

"Again?" The driver gave Mike a nasty grimace. "Go ahead and shoot. I answer only to Polzin."

Apparently the driver didn't care that he'd be answering to the devil soon if he didn't pull over. Mike heard Lauren struggling with Polzin in the back of the long car. He wanted to take a shot at the bastard but the risk to Lauren was too great. They were all dead if the driver had his way and took them over the cliff's edge.

Through the windshield there was only sky and sunshine. The incongruity of a violent death on such a clear December day burned through him. He was trained to overcome anyone in any situation. He damned sure wasn't going to die at the bottom of a cliff courtesy of an insanely loyal driver. No way. Factor in Lauren's safety and his temper hit an all-new high. He'd just found the woman—the right woman—and he wasn't about to let these human trafficking scumbags decide their fate.

The driver's jacket was soaked with blood from the bullet buried in his shoulder, but he drove as though it was nothing more than a mosquito bite.

"Brake!" Mike shouted. They were going into the curve too fast. The jerk accelerated. Left with no choice, Mike slammed the butt of the weapon into the driver's temple once, twice, then a third time. Unconscious, the man slumped over the wheel. The stubborn bastard was heavy as hell, but Mike shoved the man's foot off the gas and rammed his own against the brake, bringing the car to a stop on the right side of the road. Sirens blared and lights flashed, turning the limousine into a bad disco set as law enforcement surrounded them. Mike rammed the gearshift into park, set the gun aside, and raised his hands.

The vehicle rocked on the axles as Lauren continued her fight in the back. Mike turned, ready to kill Polzin with his bare hands for merely looking at her, but he did a double take as he surveyed the scene. Lauren wasn't in jeopardy. In fact, if someone didn't intervene quickly, Polzin would be headed for the morgue rather than a prison cell. She had Polzin pinned down and was using the knot of this tie to strangle him. His face was already mottled, his eyes wide with panic.

"Lauren, honey," Mike said quietly. "The police are here."

"I. Am. Not. Done." She punctuated each word with a squeeze of the tie around Polzin's throat.

The mobster's fingers scratched at the vise around his neck, doing more damage to his skin than the fine silk.

"We've got everything we need on him," Mike reminded her. "He won't escape."

"He killed Vanya." She squeezed again. "Killed Desmond. He would've killed you."

"I'm right here," Mike said. "Look at me, baby." She did, her gorgeous silver eyes full of grief and fury. "I'm fine and so are you."

She blinked rapidly and he watched her face transform as she realized what she was doing. "Oh!" She scooted off Polzin, over the seat, and straight into Mike's arms. "I was going to—" She clapped a hand over her mouth.

Mike gathered her close, her body trembling like a leaf in a storm. "You're going to breathe." And he was going to take his own advice and do the same.

"I could've killed him. Would have." Her breath shuddered in and out. "Happily."

"Who could blame you? Just breathe."

She buried her face in his shoulder and he felt her sucking in big gulps of air.

"You're okay." She leaned back, her hands fluttering over his face and shoulders. "You saved us!"

"I'm fine," he repeated. "You were doing a pretty good job of saving yourself."

She pushed her hair out of her face. "I wanted to kill him," she whispered, her voice quiet. "For you."

Since he'd left the Navy he couldn't think of anyone who'd cared that much about his welfare. "It's over now. The police can take it from here." He stroked a thumb across her cheekbone, and then examined her hands. Other than a swollen cheek and a couple of minor scratches, she seemed fine. "He didn't hurt you?"

"No."

"Thank God." He rubbed a hand up and down her spine, soothing them both. He'd never been more scared than when they'd tossed him into the trunk. "Just keep breathing while we talk to the police."

The responding officers dragged Polzin and his driver out of the long car, not bothering to be gentle about their injuries. When the officers asked Mike to come out of the car, he exited on the side opposite the mobsters, giving a cursory explanation of the situation. Officer Cooper joined them, a big smile on his face.

"Miss Woods, Mr. Stone, we can't thank you enough for the tip on this operation. It took some convincing, but I got the Chief of Police to listen to me rather than Treadwell. I came as soon as I could get here."

"You came," Lauren said, "that's what matters."

"You found the second car?" Mike asked.

Cooper nodded. "We did and the men are already

in custody. Why don't you let the paramedics check you out?"

"I'm good," he insisted.

"He could be bleeding internally," Lauren blurted suddenly.

Mike looked down into her worried face. "What gave you that idea?"

"P-Polzin. He said his men knew how to do that."

"He's an idiot," Mike assured her. "I know how to take a punch." What he couldn't take was one more minute holding back the words he needed to give her. "Can we have a second, Cooper?"

"Take your time. I'm not going anywhere," the officer said, that smile still on his face as he strolled away.

When they had a little privacy, Mike smiled down at her. "We did it."

"You're the real hero," Lauren said, gifting him with a soft kiss on the side of his mouth that wasn't injured.

"You're the hero." He cleared his throat. "You saved those women last night and Cooper might even be able to trace and rescue more now that you found Trinity's payment and order records. He'll probably make detective because of your help on this case."

She shivered, leaning close and lacing her fingers with his. "I wouldn't have lasted a single day without you. Cooper isn't the type to take all the credit and

I'll make sure the media gives you your due. Your dad will be so proud."

While his dad's respect would be nice, Mike was more concerned with how Lauren felt about him. She was already a media darling, this would only propel her to the limelight for all the right reasons. Could she possibly want to spend her personal time with a disgraced SEAL? "Is that a prelude to a goodbye monologue?"

Her gaze drifted away from him, out over the sweeping view. "You protected me and captured an international criminal. Your job's done. Won't the Guardian Agency assign you to another case?"

He patted his pockets. "Hard to tell. My phone's gone."

"Ha. Ha."

"For the record, as a damsel in distress, you excel at kicking ass."

She grinned. "That might be the nicest thing you've ever said to me."

He laughed. "Allow me to rectify that immediately." He cupped her face and lowered his mouth to hers, to hell with his busted lip. The kiss spun out, mesmerizing them both until they were breathless. "You're beautiful, Lauren. And a capable, amazing woman."

"*Hmm.*" She smiled. "Off to a good start."

"But I'm not absolutely sure you're safe yet." Her eyes narrowed instantly. "There could be fallout," he explained. "A misguided enforcer or two might be lurking about. I should stick around."

"You think so?" She frowned theatrically. "What aren't you telling me?"

"I will stick around," he admitted, making the decision as he said the words. He'd find a way to keep her in his life. She was nothing short of a Christmas miracle and he wasn't about to let her go. "I'm in love with you, Lauren Marie Woods, and I'm not going anywhere unless you send me away."

"I…" she swallowed. "What?"

"You heard me." He lowered his head and kissed her again. "Whatever role you play, I want to be a part of your real life. I can set up my own PI shop right here in SoCal."

Her eyes went soft, glistening with unshed tears. "Mike…"

Damn. He'd jumped in too soon. "Don't say anything now." He interrupted what he feared was a protest with another searing kiss. "Too soon, I know. Forget I said it. I'll convince you."

"Mike." She gazed up at him, and he recognized the sincerity shining in her eyes, glowing on her face. "You'll convince me to love you?" She gave a weak laugh. "Is that an order?"

"It could be," he admitted with a nod. "Hopefully I'll manage it before you ask Cooper to file a restraining order against me, but even that won't stop me."

"No, I'm sure it wouldn't."

That sounded remarkably like a compliment of his persistent, high-handed nature. And she didn't look the least bit perturbed with him. Sometimes the best option was a full frontal assault. "Assuming the best outcome here, I think we should keep the wedding small."

"Now you're planning a wedding?"

"Our wedding." He pulled her close. "A disgraced SEAL won't rate a lot of guests. Although Hank Patterson *is* a friend and he's married to Sadie McClain," he reminded her.

"Oh, I'm sure she'll want to watch a murderous, bottom of the A-list bride say her vows," Lauren said with a laugh.

"Then we'll elope. That's easier anyway."

"*Hmm.*" Her hot, silvery eyes locked with his and her fingertips lit a fire under his skin when she traced his jaw. "How about the beach at dawn?"

"Seriously?" That would be damn near perfect, though he'd happily exchange vows with her anywhere. The sooner the better. "You'd really marry me?"

"Call me convinced." Her lips curved into a sweet smile as she leaned into him. "After all, I think we've been through the worst of life. We deserve a shot at better. I love you, Mike." She kissed him softly. "I'd be honored to accept the role as Mrs. Stone."

"It's a once-in-a-lifetime part," he said, grinning

down at her. "And you're the only one who can do it." He kissed her once more. "Are you good with the traditional vows to love, honor, and obey?" He loaded that last word with plenty of innuendo.

"As long as you say them, too," she said, a wealth of mischief shining in her eyes. "I know your word is your bond."

"You have my word and… my heart." He could hardly wait to tell Hank and the rest of his friends that he'd found the love of his life in Hollywood. They'd never believe it.

With her tucked safely under his arm, they walked away from the scene, both of them eager to start building a lifetime of joy and happiness.

ABOUT REGAN BLACK

Regan Black, a USA Today and internationally best-selling author, writes award-winning, action-packed romances featuring kick-butt heroines and the sexy heroes who fall in love with them. Raised in the Midwest and California, she and her family, along with their adopted greyhound and two arrogant cats now reside in the South Carolina Lowcountry where the rich blend of legend, romance, and history fuels her imagination.

For early access to new releases, exclusive prizes, and much more, subscribe to the monthly newsletter at ReganBlack.com/perks.

Keep up with Regan online:
www.ReganBlack.com
Facebook
Twitter
Instagram

facebook.com/ReganBlack.fans

twitter.com/ReganBlack

instagram.com/reganblackauthor

ORIGINAL BROTHERHOOD
PROTECTORS SERIES

BY ELLE JAMES

Brotherhood Protectors Series

Montana SEAL (#1)

Bride Protector SEAL (#2)

Montana D-Force (#3)

Cowboy D-Force (#4)

Montana Ranger (#5)

Montana Dog Soldier (#6)

Montana SEAL Daddy (#7)

Montana Ranger's Wedding Vow (#8)

Montana SEAL Undercover Daddy (#9)

Cape Cod SEAL Rescue (#10)

Montana SEAL Friendly Fire (#11)

Montana SEAL's Bride (#12)

Montana Rescue

Hot SEAL, Salty Dog

ABOUT ELLE JAMES

ELLE JAMES also writing as MYLA JACKSON is a *New York Times* and *USA Today* Bestselling author of books including cowboys, intrigues and paranormal adventures that keep her readers on the edges of their seats. With over eighty works in a variety of sub-genres and lengths she has published with Harlequin, Samhain, Ellora's Cave, Kensington, Cleis Press, and Avon. When she's not at her computer, she's traveling, snow skiing, boating, or riding her ATV, dreaming up new stories. Learn more about Elle James at www.ellejames.com

Website | Facebook | Twitter | GoodReads | Newsletter | BookBub | Amazon

Follow Elle!
www.ellejames.com
ellejames@ellejames.com

f facebook.com/ellejamesauthor
🐦 twitter.com/ElleJamesAuthor